THE CROWHAM MARTYRS

Jane

CATNIP BOOKS
Published by Catnip Publishing Ltd
320 City Road
London
EC1V 2NZ

This edition first published 2015
1 3 5 7 9 10 8 6 4 2

A CIP catalogue record for this book is available from the British Library.

ISBN 978-1-84647-163-6

Printed and bound by CPI Group (UK) Ltd, Croydon, CR0 4YY

www.catnippublishing.co.uk

5 November. 1515

A.D.

My fingers do tremble as I write these words.

The devil liveth in yonder woods—yea, the fiend himself, who prattles and prances upon this good earth like an unholy prince.

And my heart doth weep with horror at what I have seen.

Mine own brave sister—oh, lamentable childe—to be treated thus. Like to a criminal for all thy goodness. Like to an evil witch for all thy innocence.

Never shall I speak of the tortures and cruelties that have been inflicted upon thy kindly person.

Nor speak of the infernal beast who hath these foul obscenities begot.

But never shall I forget these monstrous things, mine own dear one.

Never, ever . . .

A silver wisp of ghost hovers on the ceiling and a raspy voice rattles the timbers of my narrow staircase.

'Maddy Deeprose! You're ten minutes late.'

I run a brush through my tangled hair and look in the mirror. Pale skin, round face – shouldn't I have cheekbones by now? I'm nearly thirteen. I rummage through my dresser drawer, dig out the make-up Mum sent from the States. Maybe lipstick would help. Or some blusher. I lean into the mirror for a closer look. Thick black eyeliner?

'Seriously, Maddy, this is beyond a joke.'

'Coming, Missy.'

I slip on my blazer and stumble down from my attic room. What would be the point of having cheekbones, anyway? It's impossible to look cool in the Crowham Martyrs School uniform – a checked yellow dress, topped with an itchy blanket of dark green wool – and it's not as if anyone would notice. After all, I'm not posh or pretty, so I might as well be invisible in this place – even the ghosts ignore me.

The deputy housemistress waits at the bottom of the stairs with two bundles of school brochures and student planners. Because I've been here all summer – again – I'm helping her greet the new infants and juniors.

'And stop calling me Missy,' she growls. 'It's Miss Burke, in front of the others at least.'

When I started at Crowham two years ago, I wondered if Missy was in charge of the ghosts as well as the students. It stood to reason – the way she moved, as if she were floating. And her skin, so pale and translucent. It was in her clothes, too – gauzy and light, pastel and dreamy.

Turned out she was just a bit of a hippy, though, like an older, forty-something version of my mum. And she can't even *see* the ghosts. Nobody can, except for me.

'Come along, my dear.'

She pats me on the back and whisks me along the corridor. I get a whiff of tobacco and her old-fashioned patchouli perfume. On most people the scent would be overkill, but on Missy it's just right, a bit exotic, like spices from a street market in Marrakech or Istanbul, not that I've ever been to those places . . .

'Any news from La-la land?'

Missy tosses the question while we scuttle down the newly polished parquet floor, trying not to slip.

'Mum's a doctor at the moment.'

'At least she's off the streets for a change,' Missy replies. 'What was she the last time? A drug dealer?'

'Something worse, I'm afraid.'

Missy laughs and smiles at me, and for a few seconds, I don't feel so alone.

Mum's an actress, living in Los Angeles – far, far away. She started out with smallish parts on British TV – historical dramas, mostly. 'I've got a face for bonnets,' she'd say. They were nice, the bonnet years – the late night line-learning in our cosy London flat, the early morning breakfasts before the studio's driver arrived, the school around the corner where I got dropped off every day.

Missy glides along the corridor and down the mezzanine staircase so gracefully you'd think she could slip between the cracks the way the ghosts do. As we pass the huge fireplace by the front door I catch a glimpse of one, two, maybe three of them – they're so close together it's like counting clouds in an overcast sky – hovering near the heating vent, ready to swirl away.

The ghosts never cause me any problems, though.

Think of the sound a radio makes when it's not tuned in properly. It's just background noise, right? Annoying, but a person can live with it. That's what the ghosts are like – most of them, anyway; a kind of visible static that I can't completely turn off or clearly tune into.

Okay, there was *one* ghost when we first got to LA, who was clearer than the others. I called her Edwina. She crouched in the stairwell of our run-down apartment building. She had something like a face – that was weird – and it seemed bruised and puffy, as if she'd been stuck under water when she was alive, as if somebody had deliberately –

'Hurry, Maddy.' Missy waits impatiently at the front door. 'We don't want the little ones to wet themselves while they're waiting, do we?'

Then Mum met Robert, a big time Hollywood producer, and it was bye-bye Edwina, bye-bye rat-infested neighbourhood, and hello glass-fronted house in Hollywood Hills.

Robert's money wasn't important to me, though. His pool and Jacuzzi meant nothing, those ceiling-high windows overlooking Los Angeles only made me feel dizzy and anxious, like there was nothing between me and the rest of the world.

So when I got shipped back to England just a few weeks after we moved in with Robert – when Mum dumped me at the Crowham Martyrs Boarding Kennel without a word of explanation – who cared? Not me.

Mum was happy with Robert; she was safe in that luxurious house up in the hills.

And the ghosts here at Crowham never bothered me in the slightest. Because they're nothing, really, just like poor old Edwina.

You can't be afraid of *nothing*, right?

A crop of eager faces sways on the lawn, like dwarf sunflowers in a field.

'Hel-lo!' Mr Grayling, the headmaster, bellows, shaking hands with one of the parents.

'Good-morn-ing!'

The gentle breeze has blown his comb-over off course so his head gleams in the sunlight. He's wearing his dark suit even though it's as warm as a summer day. It's all such a performance – the caterers and cleaners are lined up like an honour guard in their starched black dresses and white aprons. Who is the school trying to fool?

On the gravel drive, the cars – silver Mercs, chrome blue BMWs – honk and strain to make their escapes. It's a quick enough procedure – drop off little darling, shake somebody's hand, head off back to the country pile or the island in the Caribbean – but they're still in a mad rush to get away.

'Maddy! You are needed!'

Missy stands behind a makeshift bar, pouring champagne into fluted glasses that have been arranged on a tray.

'We need to find little Jordan,' Missy whispers. 'He's here somewhere.'

'Who?'

Somebody's pink-shirted bull of a father swaggers up to the table and takes a glass from Missy's tray. She glowers at him, but he downs the champagne in one frothy gulp and struts back to his wife – an orange, overstretched skeleton in jeans and Chanel.

'Jordan Fairlight.' Missy picks up the dirty glass, gives it a quick wipe with a tea towel. 'New boy in Year 3. I told you about him yesterday, remember? Showed you his picture?'

I look across the lawn for a boy with blond curls and piercing blue eyes that are the right side of creepy, but only just.

'Go find him,' Missy says. 'He arrived on his own and needs looking after.'

I put my brochures down and weave through the crowd. As I step on to the gravel drive, something bright reflects off the bumper of a parked car, dazzling me. A metallic bronze Mercedes pulls into the driveway and a tinted window rolls down.

Natalie Ashmore – self-crowned queen of Crowham – is back. After her chauffeur stops the car, she gets out and glances around as if she's expecting to be mobbed by a crowd of photographers.

I wave cheerfully and smile. She sees me, she must do – and she recognises me, because we're in the same house – but her eyes glaze over, and she stumbles forward, on the lookout for someone more interesting, more popular.

Who needs her, I think, as I tromp down to the bottom of the driveway, swallowing the embarrassment and hurt. *Who needs anybody at this stupid school?*

Another car pulls through the front gate – a massive silver Audi – and I have to step aside. I check the pavements on the other side of the school walls, look up and down for Jordan Fairlight.

Nothing. Nobody. Where has he gone?

Across the road Crowham Wood looms like something out of a Grimms' fairy tale, with tall, thick spruces and firs growing on the fringes, forming an almost impenetrable barrier.

The day after I arrived at Crowham – on my own, like Jordan, but without any champagne reception because it was the middle of the term and the dead of night – Missy made a huge show of leading me through the gates, marching me across the road, forcing me to stand at the edge of the forest and gaze into the shadows. *Think how terrified you'd be if you got lost in there, Maddy*, she said. *Imagine how long it would take for you to be found.*

Two years later, the darkness and cold still make me shiver. There's no way Jordan would have wandered into Crowham Wood on his own – not if he'd heard of Hansel and Gretel, or the Big Bad Wolf, anyway.

I head back towards the refreshments table, scanning each new face. There's a pudgy little girl with her hair in pink-ribboned bunches; there's a boy who's sobbing and clinging on to his weeping mother's yellow and gold sari.

And on the lawn, there's a blond kid, gazing up at the school, his mouth wide open, his eyes filled with terror. He's shaking too, and who could blame him? The gaping mouth of the school's front door, the blank stares of the windows, the jagged crown of spikes along the rooftop – the school looks like a monster ready to gobble up a child-sized treat.

'Jordan?'

'Y-y-yes?'

Jordan's staring at a row of stained-glass windows above the main entrance, dazzlingly lit by the sun's light.

I squint to block the harsh rays, but I can't see anything scary.

'Don't worry,' I say. 'The building only *looks* like it bites.'

Suddenly, Jordan gets worse – his teeth chatter, his head

twitches from side to side and his body shakes as if he's having a seizure or some bizarre reaction to the light.

Before I have a chance to shout for help, Missy's at my side. 'Jordan?'

He's still trembling, transfixed. I glance up again – what is he afraid of? There's just the sunlight glinting off bright coloured glass.

Missy stoops over and puts her arms around Jordan's shoulders. 'It's all right, dear,' she purrs. 'You're bound to be upset on your first day, but that will soon pass.' Her voice is calm and reassuring, and soon she straightens up, waiting for him to calm down. She smiles at him, sighing patiently, and pats his shoulder while she glances back across the lawn and up at the windows.

We stand still, waiting for Jordan's noisy sobs to subside.

Missy hardly moves, so at first I don't notice what she's doing.

She's watching the building. I can only see it from the corner of my eyes, but her chin is tilting slightly and her eyes move upwards. She's scanning the top of the roof – the slate tiles, the lead seams, the tall brick chimney.

What is she looking for?

'Right then.' Missy claps her hands briskly, and Jordan finally snaps out of it. 'Lunchtime. We can't keep Mrs Gibson waiting.'

She pats Jordan on the shoulder and guides his faltering steps towards the front door. I follow behind, checking out those windows before Missy can turn around and see me.

There *is* something, barely visible at one of the narrow panes. It's not a ghost. It doesn't have a form or a shape, it's just a dull, glowing wash of grey, like dark light, like –

'Maddy,' Missy barks. '*Do* try to keep up.'

Like nothing I've seen before.

The clouds are heavy with rain and threatening thunder. I'm high above the ocean, standing on the edge of a grassy outcrop – scared to look down, but unable to resist a quick glance at the boiling foam that bashes against the rocks below.

'Maddy, get away from there.'

Mum's voice is harsh, anxious.

'Now!'

I inch backwards on to solid ground, holding out my arms for balance.

Something touches me.

A hand – rough and leathery – grabs my wrist, squeezes until it hurts. I look up – who is this? Who's dragging me along the clifftop's jagged edge? I can't see anything in the mist and rain. I can only feel the hand, pulling me faster and faster until everything swirls together in a terrifying blur – the angry sea, the scowling horizon, the crumbling path beneath my feet –

The alarm clangs. I bundle the duvet around my neck, check the time.

I try to remember the nightmare. At least I think that's what it was – the sea, a clifftop, somewhere familiar. Have I been there? Or just dreamed about it before?

It takes a few seconds before I realise how quiet – how *weirdly* quiet – it is this morning. Normally on the first day of term there'd be loads of noise from downstairs – girls rushing about getting ready, the prefects barking out orders, footsteps thundering down the hallway for the first breakfast sitting or racing back and forth between the rooms.

I push the duvet down and look around my room. The shelf in the corner is still listing to the left. The posters Mum sent to remind me of the West Coast – paintings by Hockney and Kahlo and O'Keefe – are still Blu-tacked to the sloping attic wall, brightening the room like rays of Californian sunshine. Sweet wrappers and empty drinks cans are strewn across my desk and clothes tuft out of part-opened drawers . . .

Everything's the same, isn't it?

Of course it is. It was just that creepy dream, Maddy, so pull yourself together. There's nothing in your room that's going to grab you or drag you along the top of a cliff or –

I hear a scraping sound. Then another, and another like a series of tiny scratches. Where is it coming from? There are no ghosts trying to find a way up through the ceiling, no tree branches or telephone wires are tapping at the window. What about the wardrobe? Is something inside it, trying to claw its way out?

Footsteps creak on my staircase and something shuffles outside my door.

'H-h-hello?' It's a squeaky whisper.

I pull the duvet back up, gather it around my throat, as if that could smother my panic and stifle the sounds of my thumping heart. Who could this be? None of the other girls ever comes up to my room, so is it one of the ghosts? But they can't talk . . .

More shuffling from behind the door, an almost silent tap-tap-tap.

'M-M-Maddy?'

My stomach flips. *It knows my name.*

'Are you there?'

Finally, I get out of bed. I put on my dressing gown and tiptoe to the door – one step, two steps, three steps, four. My hands shake, and my muscles are tight with a fear I've never felt at Crowham before.

'L-let me in, Maddy. Please.'

I take a deep breath. The door groans on its hinges as I open it enough to peek through the narrow gap, dreading some ghost child's translucent face or a monster's grip finding my wrist . . .

There's a kid at the door all right. Jordan Fairlight, the Year 3 boy, alive and well and looking as frightened as I am.

'You were m-meant to take me around,' he stutters.

Suddenly I remember – Missy asked me to give him a tour of the school before assembly, show him the ropes, do the whole big sister routine.

'And then I couldn't find you . . . and . . . and then . . .' He whips his head around, as if someone's waiting at the bottom of the stairs.

'Those *fings*,' Jordan whispers.

I glance behind him – no one's there – and pull him into my room, closing the door and locking it, just in case.

'Th-those *fings* won't let me b-be,' he blubs.

His head jerks back and forth, as if he's trying to get rid of a bad memory.

'*Fings*, Jordan?' I demand. 'What's a *fing*?'

'Those *fings*.' He wipes his damp eyes on the back of his blazer cuff. 'Those ones that come out of the walls.'

A ghost sweeps under the door. It whooshes up to the top of the ceiling, dropping down to the mirror where it twists and twirls, like it's trying out some new dance moves.

Jordan lets out a cry and grabs me by the legs as the ghost floats through the window, leaving nothing behind but a owing spot of smudgy darkness embedded in the mirror. What is that? I wonder. Ghost poo?

Jordan lets out a massive, shuddery sigh.

'What *things*?' I ask.

When I glance at the mirror again, the weird stain is gone.

Jordan sniffs. '*Fings* that want to hurt me.'

4

Mrs Gibson, the head cook, scowls behind the serving table, her massive bosoms bristling underneath a stained blue and white tabard.

The dining hall's empty except for Jordan and me, and the long wobbly tables are strewn with dirty plates and half-empty cereal bowls. Cutlery and wadded up serviettes litter the floor. The sound of Jordan's clinking teacup bounces off the smooth, plastered walls and echoes up to the oak-beamed ceiling.

'Do you know where your form room is, Jordan?' I try to sound kind and caring, but I *so* don't want to be late for registration on the first day of term. 'We've missed the start of assembly, but we could sneak you –'

Jordan lets out a little sob.

'Who's your form tutor? Can you remember the name?'

No words, just a twitch and a sniff. I sift through the rubbish on the table, find him a clean-ish serviette.

Maybe now would be the time to talk to him about the ghosts – they *must* be the things he sees. I've seen ghosts for years, I could say. They've followed me, like weird but harmless shadows, from London to LA, and they were waiting for me when I got to Crowham. And I'm not a freak, am I? I'm almost one hundred per cent normal, and that's a fact.

But of course I don't tell him about the ghosts. I *can't* tell him. I can't tell *anyone*.

Never, ever.

Finally, Jordan blows his nose and picks up his bag. As I lead him away from the table he looks around – up at the ceiling, along the row of narrow stained-glass windows that line the walls, back at the red-faced Mrs Gibson.

'Off you go!' she shouts. There's a sharpness to her voice, a nasty scratching like the steel wool she uses to scrape out pots and pans. As we hurry out of the room, the door slams behind us, knocking us into the narrow, gloomy corridor.

'That Mrs Gibson is a witch,' Jordan whispers.

'You're probably right,' I laugh, but Jordan's already distracted by something new. He's looking up at the walls, wide-eyed, terrified. And it's no wonder – portraits of long-dead headmasters and bursars glare down at us with scowling, whiskery faces.

'They're only pictures, Jordan,' I say.

We stop and look. 'This one's called Obadiah Dimwilly,' I say. It's close enough to the real thing.

The man in the next picture looks like the headmaster, Mr Grayling, after he's been mummified and had a top hat put on his head.

'What about this one?' Jordan asks.

'Let's see.' I stand on my tiptoes, make a big show of squinting my eyes so I can read the name. 'Wolfgang von Bumkisser.'

Jordan pulls a face. 'You're silly.'

'And I'm very, very late, so let's get moving.'

We reach the main entrance hall and Jordan gawps at the massive space – the cave-sized fireplace, the huge stained-glass window, the wide oak stairs that curl up to the top of the room, creating a long mezzanine.

He takes my hand again, clutches it tight. 'M-Maddy?'

He stares at the ceiling. I look up at the high-windowed dome, but there's no sign of those strange, dark smudges. There's only the usual cluster of ghosts, swirling like strands of candy floss.

I kneel beside Jordan, look him in the eye. 'It's okay,' I whisper. 'I get frightened sometimes, too.'

'You *do*?'

23

'Of course,' I say, looking up at the ceiling, giving his hand a big-sisterly squeeze. 'Ghosts can be scary.'

As soon as I say *ghost* the floor begins to rumble.

I panic for a second – I shouldn't have said the word – but it's just some Year 11 boys who've pushed their way through the assembly hall door, and are shoving and jostling towards us on their way to lessons. When the crowd thins we slip behind the students who stroll towards the humanities rooms in groups of twos and threes.

'You're funny,' Jordan giggles.

I pull him along, thinking about how weird this all is. A minute ago he was paralysed with fear, and now . . .

'There's no such thing as ghosts,' he laughs. 'Everybody knows that.'

Mr Casey's a legend. First history lesson of term and he's already ranting.

'The spectacles of hate are nothing new,' he bellows, karate-chopping the air with each syllable.

He's flung his jacket on to the back of his chair and is waving his arms and shaking his head, so his grey curls bounce like springs. We're meant to be studying the Tudors and Stuarts – Henry VIII, Bloody Mary, King James and all that – but he's gone off topic as usual.

'Have a look at this image from 1547.'

On the wonky whiteboard screen there's an etching of four dead women hanging from a wide gallows, suspended by ropes around their necks. They've been executed for being witches – a horrible, terrifying death – but by the looks on their faces you'd think they're just waiting for the man in the corner of the picture to climb his ladder and cut them down. That they'll thank him when he does, tip him a few pennies.

'The courtyard of York Minster,' Mr Casey says. His voice sounds choked, emotional. Is he going to cry?

'According to historical evidence – in this case an etching made at the time – who might we say was hated by society in 1547?'

He scans the room, but nobody says anything. Jaws hang open – no one knows the answer, including me, although I manage to keep my mouth closed.

'Was it women, Sir?'

Everyone turns around or strains forward to look at the girl in the third row who gave the answer. It's not me, of course – it's the new student from South Africa, who's sitting at the desk beside mine.

'Your name's Hannah – is that right?' Mr Casey goes back to his desk, checks the register that he'd forgotten to take. 'Hannah Masupha-Harris?'

'Yes, Sir,' she mutters. 'Sorry for shouting out.'

'Never mind, Hannah. Your answer was good.'

He goes back to his slide show, zooms in on the etching.

'It wasn't just women of course, and it wasn't all of them, but when we look at the picture we can see that some women were targeted – called witches – because they were feared. Their sexuality gave them power over men, so if they couldn't be controlled through marriage . . .'

When Mr Casey says 'sexuality', the boys in the back of the class laugh and snigger. Hannah looks across the aisle, her mouth turned up in a sneaky, secret smile. She rolls her eyes at me and I roll mine right back.

Mr Casey changes the slide. This picture's more detailed – tied-up men on slabs are being dragged behind horses, while in the distance one man is hanged and another man's guts are being pulled from a huge open wound.

'That's disgusting, Sir,' says one of the boys.

'Tyburn Hill, London. 1606. Recognise the face of the man on the gallows?'

Mr Casey's voice sounds cheerier than when he was showing us the witches. 'Bit of a celebrity here in Crowham?' He waits a few seconds, zooms the picture so that we can see a peaked cap, a pointy moustache and a narrow chin. '*Remember, remember, the fifth of November?*'

Mr Casey strolls between the desks and sighs at our lack of enthusiasm.

'Guy Fawkes, ladies and gentlemen. Now a symbol of opposition everywhere, and whose effigy will, in several weeks' time, be paraded down Crowham High Street and burned on a pyre in Market Square.'

Mr Casey stops beside Jake Coates' desk. Jake's head has dropped on to his chin and he's drooling, fast

27

asleep. Mr Casey leans over him.

'So, what religious group did King James – and much of British society – fear and hate in 1606? Mr Coates?'

Jake starts awake. 'Huh?'

'I asked a question – who did English society most fear and loathe in the year 1606?'

Jake wipes his eyes like a sleeping baby.

'Jake?'

'Dunno, Sir . . . was it you?'

The classroom erupts with laughter. Mr Casey makes a fist and pretends to give Jake a bash on the head.

'Catholics.' Mr Casey shrieks over the din and strides back to the front of the room. 'Members of the Roman Catholic Church, who were oppressed and aggrieved to such an extent that they –' and he's off again. Another slide. Another shocking image from the past, more cheers and whoops from the boys in the back, as the pictures get bloodier and more gruesome.

Mr Casey finally stops, ready to explain something – what 'quartering' means, though the picture he's showing does that well enough. Somebody behind me groans at the image. I feel it too, but isn't that Sir's point? To upset us? To shake things up? To make us think?

In the etching someone's being cut up like a joint of meat by men with huge axes. People in the background are watching

– there's a man in the shadows who smiles to himself, as if he thinks it's all a joke. I stare at his face – he's got dark hair and black eyes and somehow, in this four-hundred-year-old etching, he looks strangely familiar.

The groaning behind me gets louder.

'Turn that off, Sir,' somebody shouts.

Mr Casey goes back to the first slide, to the women on the scaffold who look so cheerful and content. But the groaning – is that what it is? – gets louder, deeper, *weirder*. When I turn around to see who's making the noise, a horde of ghosts swoops under the door, between the floorboards, through the windows. I've never seen so many – they're like a thick fog, making everything blurry. What's going on?

I try to stay focused on the lesson. Mr Casey's still going on about Bonfire Night – who will this year's guest effigy be? A benefits claimant? An immigrant?

Chairs scrape the floor and I can hear Mr Casey's words over the strange groaning sounds – 'Get into your groups, boys and girls.' As desks are shoved together I hear Jake say, 'I don't want to sit next to her, Sir'. I know he's talking about me, but I don't even care. I should push my chair back like everyone else – but I can't move.

The groaning becomes deafening, and it's not the only sound. I put my hands up over my ears but it's no protection from what

I'm hearing – a deep grinding, like a huge rusty engine that can't quite start up, and dry crackles like a raging fire.

'Sorry, but are you all right?'

A girl's voice reaches me through the haze of horrible noise. A hand grips my shoulder. I try to focus on her face, but there's just a dim grey light, a mist of ghosts, and beyond them, an untouchable layer of darkness.

'Sir, I don't think this girl's feeling very well.'

Anything that's solid moves away. The students – falling over their desks, tipping their chairs – stand back, leaving the ghosts to fill the empty spaces like cold cotton wool, softening my fall.

'Hurry, Sir – she's having some sort of seizure.'

And then it's over.

Everything's black.

I'm gone.

6

Bare walls. A tiny white bed. A single wooden chair. Shards of sunlight through a narrow leaded window.

No sounds. No people.

I'm dead, right? And this is, like, heaven?

I swallow. Breathe. Breathing – that's a good sign.

'Hello?' My voice croaks as if I haven't used it for years.

Or maybe I've been in a coma. I touch my arms, my face, my hair – everything feels normal. I cup my hands, bring them to my mouth and blow.

Warmth.

And outside the room, sounds. Footsteps. Voices – more than one, I think – whispering harshly.

I feel my heart beating in my chest, so I must be alive – unless it's like one of those phantom limb things where your leg's been cut off but it doesn't stop hurting. Maybe the dead don't realise what's happened to them. Maybe they still feel their heartbeats, still sweat with panic and shake with fear.

The door opens.

I smell her patchouli perfume before I see her. Missy sweeps in, her arms laden with carrier bags and a green rucksack – mine – that dangles open at her side.

'Well, that's a fine start to the term, Maddy Deeprose.'

She pulls up the chair and slings the rucksack on to the end of the bed.

'I've seen all your teachers and explained that you feel unwell.' She takes out a history book, holds it up for me to see. 'Here's this morning's homework assignment from Mr Casey – I think he's in worse shape than you, poor thing. He was as white as a sheet by the time Matron and I arrived at his classroom. I daresay he won't be teaching *that* particular lesson again soon.'

She rifles through my bag, looking for more homework, all the time humming to herself, rustling pieces of paper.

'Here it is.' She pulls a sheet of lined paper out of the bag. 'English. Two hundred words on imagery in *Dulce et Decorum est* . . .'

A ghost slips through the window in an odd jerky movement, as if it's being pulled along by a string. I glance at it for a second – without moving my head – but when I look at back at Missy, she's watching my face, her eyes narrowed.

I smile at her, my heart pounding. She doesn't know about

the ghosts, does she? She *can't* know.

Suddenly, I remember Jordan – the *fings* he saw and how terrified he was.

'Jordan,' I splutter. 'I was supposed to meet him after school.'

Missy moves closer to the bed. 'There's no need to worry,' she purrs. 'I'm taking care of both of you now.'

'Well, at least tell him I'm sorry,' I say. 'I don't want him to feel like he's been abandoned.'

Missy repacks my bag and puts it on the chair beside my bed. 'Abandoned,' she says. 'Oh, you are funny, Madeline.'

Madeline? Nobody calls me that, not even Mum.

She leans over me, pats my shoulder. I pull away slightly – she's not going to kiss me, is she? 'No one's ever abandoned at Crowham,' she says with a raspy chuckle. 'There's always *some*body looking after you – whether you like it or not.'

As soon as Missy's gone I hear the ghost, scratching on the ceiling, as if it's trying to get my attention. It's pretty, this one – it has a silvery misty tail, with tiny glitter flecks. Funny I never noticed it before. *Who were you?* I want to ask. *Why are you here?*

Mum used to call the ghosts my invisible friends. She made jokes about them, like she thought it was cute. But then I got too old for invisible friends, and if I mentioned them in public, Mum's face would get red and she'd squeeze my hand. Once when I didn't shut up straight away, she dragged me out to the pavement by the wrist and pinched me until I cried.

'Do you want people to think I'm a bad mother?' she sobbed. 'A bad mother with a crazy daughter who sees things that don't exist?'

At first I thought she was angry, but the way she was shaking, the way her eyes darted back and forth, it was more like she was scared someone had heard me.

'Don't talk about the ghosts, Maddy.'

She hugged me, sobbing into my hair. 'Never, ever, darling.'

'Never, ever,' I whispered.

She let up her grip for a second. She gazed into my eyes, her face wet with tears.

'Swear you won't,' she whispered hoarsely. 'Swear on your mother's life.'

'But isn't swearing bad?'

'Not *this* swearing, darling. This is different – like a promise. So just say the words . . .'

She dug her fingers into my shoulders and shook me. Harder and harder, not stopping until I said the words, made the promise.

Until I finally swore on my mother's life.

Outside my room, soft footsteps approach the door. There's a gentle knock, and a smiling face appears in the doorway.

'Hey.' It's Hannah Masupha-Harris, the girl from history. She's carrying a glass tumbler full of the yellow and white daisies that grow in thick clumps around the school. She's added long leaves of bright green grass, made them look pretty – special, somehow.

'Miss Burke said I shouldn't stay very long.'

'She fusses too much,' I say. 'I'm fine.'

'Really?' Hannah puts the flowers on my bedside table.

I shrug. 'You were there when I fainted.'

'Seemed like more than that.' She looks around, squinting, as if there's something in the room that she can't quite see.

'Well, it wasn't,' I say.

'You looked so terrified. The expression on your face, it was –'

'I fainted.' The words come out a little harsher than I mean them to. 'I blacked out – that was all.'

'I was worried,' Hannah says, fiddling with the flowers. 'I meet somebody who seems cool, who I want to make friends with, and a few minutes later, she collapses.'

Cool? Is that what she just said? *Friends?*

She laughs. 'Wondered if I was a jinx or something.'

Hannah glances around the room again, shaking her head. 'What a weird old building, eh?'

I nod.

'Whole school gives me the creeps. I don't know what possessed my parents to send me *here*. They said it was to keep me safe – whatever that means – but this place is like something out of the Dark Ages. No wi-fi, and having to use *payphones*? I didn't think they even made those things any more.'

'It's to do with the woods,' I say. 'No mobile reception. The trees are too tall.'

Hannah sighs. 'That's what they tell us, anyway.'

She goes to the window and cranes her neck to see outside.

'Though, I've got to admit, those tress *are* pretty massive. I don't think I've ever seen any that size, at least not in England.'

There's a knock on the door, and Matron pops her head in.

'Rest time,' she growls. 'You have to go.'

Hannah gives her a little wave, and Matron pads out on heavy-soled shoes, her shoulders sloped, her beefy arms dangling at her sides.

'See what I mean?' Hannah says. 'Even the school nurse looks like Frankenstein's monster.'

I start to giggle, and Matron pops an angry face in the doorway again and clears her throat.

'We'll talk later.' Hannah whispers into my ear as she air

kisses my cheeks. 'You take care now.' She says it loudly, so that Matron can hear. 'No more of your *fainting*, okay?'

Matron waits for Hannah to leave, and closes the door, leaving behind a massive silence and a whirlwind of confusion. I think about what Hannah said – that I was cool, for one thing; that Crowham was creepy, for another.

My heart's pounding, too. It was like she didn't believe that I'd just fainted, like she thought there was more to it. But she was there – she saw the same pictures, she must have felt upset, too. Others must have felt sick and woozy at the sight of that gore; it couldn't have been just me.

Suddenly, I hear Mum's voice in my head.

Never talk about the ghosts, Maddy.

As if, I think. I fainted, that's all – this had nothing to do with the stupid ghosts.

Never ever, Maddy.

Yeah, yeah, I heard you the first time.

On your mother's life.

I pull up the covers, wrap myself as tightly as I can, but I feel cold and empty now that I'm alone again, as hollowed-out as the ghost over my bed. I look up at it – at *her*. It's the pretty, silvery one again, glittering and swirling in a translucent circle. She sounds lovely, too – like a distant sea, softly whooshing, soothing me to sleep.

It's still dark when I wake up, and there's a terrible howling outside the sick room. My breathing's fast and shallow and my nightdress is soaked with sweat.

I sit up, push away the duvet. No, too cold. I pull it back up to my chin, shivering.

I had that nightmare again – the same, but different. I was being dragged and pulled, but there weren't any crashing waves this time, there wasn't a cliff. There was just hard ground. Frozen mud beneath my numb, bare feet and –

A gust of wind batters the school's stone walls – that must be what woke me – and the chimney groans as if it's about to topple over and crash through the ceiling.

I switch on the bedside lamp. The low-watt bulb creates a comforting glow. The wind dies down, but the sound is still loud enough to drown out any footsteps – this would be the perfect time to make a run for it, go back to my attic room where it's warm and safe.

I get out of bed and slip into the dressing gown that's hanging on the back of the door. I pull the hood up over my head, Red Riding Hood-style. I stop in the doorway, holding on to the frame, taking a deep breath to calm myself.

It takes a few seconds, but I'm ready to move. After all, what's there to be afraid of? Weird dreams aren't reality. The storm outside is just light and noise. And those ghosts on the ceiling? They're nothing more than the vaporous remains of the dead, floating, flying . . .

I peer up and down the corridor. To my right, the dim light fades and the narrow hallway becomes an endless tunnel of nothingness. It leads to another back staircase – I know that, I've been down there loads of times during the day, even though the sign outside Matron's door says: *No students beyond this point* – but tonight the darkness seems to move, and I hear a raspy, scratchy breath . . .

Matron snoring from across the hall, Maddy. Get a grip!

I look the other way, where a row of wall sconces makes it easier to see. Silently, I creep along the corridor, clinging to the wall for balance and strength. I reach the end, and turn on to the wide landing that leads to the mezzanine above the entrance hall. The first of the arched windows – the one that Jordan gazed up at in horror – is in front of me, to my left, but there's no dark, glowing stain. The sky is on fire with electricity

39

– huge forks of lightning cut through the blackness like jagged flames.

A thunderclap shakes the building, and I flatten myself against the wall. A woman screams – is *that* real? Who could it be?

Over the thunder's rumbling tail an angry fist thumps against a heavy door, and I hear the crackle of flames – too loud for any fireplace. And what's that other sound? It's like a wooden gallows, creaking as a dangling body weighs it down, swaying back and forth, back and forth.

I crouch down and clap my hands over my ears, but the noises get worse. Women weep and wail and I hear mumbled words – like droning prayers in a language I don't understand. The smells are sickening, too – dense smoke, burning flesh, sweat and grime of dirty straw clinging to a filthy dress that I can feel against my –

Something bright, almost blinding, flares across the shiny floor below me. A sudden flash skims the walls, then shoots away – hot white light that's gone in a second, leaving me trembling in the darkness.

Headlights. A car.

Everything's quiet. No more screaming, no more horrible smells.

Outside, footsteps crunch on the gravel path. A fist bangs

on the front door – a real fist this time, an actual door. The dim wall lights flicker back into life. The crystals in the main chandelier glow like pale yellow embers.

Another thump on the door. Then four hard knocks that set my pulse racing again.

I force myself to stand up straight and take a deep breath. I need to get back to my bedroom, that's all. Back to reality. It's only metres ahead of me – through the double doors, down the corridor, up the narrow stairs.

There's another groaning sound from below, as the front door opens on heavy hinges, and scrapes across the marble floor. A figure looms in the doorway. It's indistinct, like a shadow – slouching, hump-backed, man-sized.

I step away from the wall and my eyes widen, straining to see, as the figure straightens, moves into the room and stands under the chandelier, bathed in amber light.

No. He's not some kind of monster, or even a man. He's just a boy in jeans and hoodie, carrying a rucksack on his back. As he walks across the floor, his footsteps are like perfectly rhythmic drum beats. He laughs when he trips up on the edge of the carpet and his voice is deep and rich.

Then he stands still, and my heart stops with him. He turns his head – looks around the room, casting his eyes to the domed ceiling, the huge windows, the landing. It's as if he's been here before, and is trying to find something he recognizes. He lifts his head, towards where I'm standing.

I slink back to the wall, tighten the cord on my dressing gown.

The chandelier light catches his face, sparking against the brilliant whites of his eyes. He's holding still, so I have time to take in his handsome features. I raise my hand, push the hood of my dressing gown away from my face. The boy reaches up, like I'm doing, and lowers his hood, too.

His hair springs out, long dark curls bounce on to his wide shoulders.

I smile. I can't help myself.

The boy does the same – looks up in my direction, smiles. Why is he doing that? Can he see me? It's as if we're linked somehow, connected by an invisible string. I move, he moves. I smile, so does he.

Under the mezzanine, a door squeaks open and soft footsteps shuffle across the marble floor. Before I see who it is, or hear any words, I smell Missy's perfume. Silently, she takes the boy's rucksack. He's still staring at me, and her eyes follow his.

I hold my breath.

'What?' Missy whispers.

He reaches up and covers his head again.

Missy sighs indulgently. 'Come on,' she says, 'you're late.'

The boy doesn't move. Just looks at me and smiles.

No. I'm imagining things. He can't actually see me. Not from down there – of course he can't.

'Caleb,' Missy whispers hoarsely. 'I want to get some sleep.'

He tugs at his hood, takes his rucksack from Missy.

'Caleb! Hurry.'

A final glance, and then he's gone, through the doors, down the corridor to the boys' dorms.

Missy dims the lights as she leaves. As soon as she's gone the horrible noises start again. The desperate shrieks seem to chase me across the landing, but as I stumble forward, there's another sound in my head.

A name.

Caleb.

I say it in my head over and over, until it drowns out the screams, muffles the sobs.

Caleb, Caleb, Caleb.

The assembly hall's full. I'm perched on a hard, narrow bench, squashed between Hannah and one of the senior prefects who's taken out his black book and is writing down the name of anyone who's talking or fidgeting or breathing too much.

It's hot in here, too – outside, after the storm, it's a perfect autumn day, but here in the airless hall, the smell of sweat and cheap body spray spreads like an invisible fog.

Down the line, somebody farts. A bench clears, nearly toppling over the kids who can't get out of the way in time. A gangly boy takes out a deodorant can and assaults the air with an even more toxic scent.

Nat Ashmore is far away from the stink and stupidity, naturally. She's perched on the stage at the end of the room with the visiting VIPs – Reverend Anne, the young vicar from St Michael's Church in Crowham village, and a purple-haired old lady who's the head of the Crowham Bonfire Planning Committee.

And who is sitting next to Nat?

Long tendrils of black hair. Shoulders so broad his school blazer strains at the seams. Eyes – huge, bright blue.

Of course the new boy would go for Nat. Of course those upward looks last night had nothing to do with me. He didn't even see me – how could he, in the dark? – much less smile at me. And if he had seen me, well, there's no way the most gorgeous boy in Crowham history – and a Year 10 at that – would ever be interested.

Hannah leans into me. 'Who's the divine creature on the stage?'

'Name's Caleb, I think.' I try to sound cool, uninterested. 'He got here last night. During the storm.'

Hannah sighs, like I imagine every other girl in the room is doing, along with some of the boys. 'I wonder why he's here,' she whispers dramatically. 'Do you think he's, like, an orphan or something?'

I tsk and roll my eyes. 'An orphan? *Really?* Can't you do better than that?

'Okay, then, maybe he got expelled from another school for doing something really, really . . . ' Hannah lowers her voice so that it's a husky purr, ' . . . bad.'

The back doors open and the headmaster strides into the room, the academic gown over his suit billowing out like bat wings. The other teachers trail behind him and spread out through the hall in a pincer-like movement. They take position in the aisles – in front of us, behind us, beside us – staring, tutting, pointing out Year 7 kids who aren't sitting *completely* still or haven't got their ties on *exactly* straight.

From the corner of my eye I see Jordan sitting across the aisle. Missy stands near him, straight-backed, her eyes fixed on the stage. Mr Casey's on my side of the room, along with Mrs Gibson, the head cook and part-time enforcer, and other members of staff.

'Good morning, students.' Mr Grayling adjusts the mike on his lectern. 'Several announcements before we begin our second day of the new term. The Bonfire Committee has its first meeting after school in the senior student common room, immediately after last lesson. Natalie Ashmore will be organising this year's event and I know she's looking to recruit some fresh blood . . .'

There's a commotion to my right. Heads turn, and some of the Year 8s stand up to see what's going on.

'Look,' Hannah says, leaning across me to get a better look. 'That little boy.'

Students are pushing back chairs and benches, clearing an area on the floor, where Jordan is lying flat out.

'It's like yesterday, when you collapsed,' Hannah whispers.

I stand up and push toward the aisle, but Missy's there in an instant. She scoops Jordan into her arms and whisks him out the door.

The headmaster doesn't drop a word.

'As I was saying, the Bonfire Committee's meetings will begin this week, and this marks the start of . . .'

He drones on and on, and I shuffle back to my seat. Hannah looks at me, raising her eyebrows, as if to say, 'see what I mean about Crowham being creepy?'

And it is creepy. Everyone's listening attentively, their backs straight and their eyes forward. A teacher carries out an unconscious child, who could be dead or dying, and nobody chatters? Nobody asks questions? Nobody turns around in their seats to see where he's gone?

Maybe it's always been like this, maybe I've just never noticed it before.

But I keep still, too, and pretend to listen. I try not to think about what happened to Jordan, or how everybody's behaving, or the other weird stuff that's been going on.

I try not to think about Caleb, either, up there on the stage with his beautiful eyes. The way I felt last night – as if I knew him. As if I'd known him all my life.

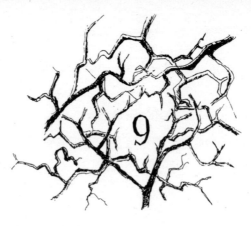

'The real world!' Hannah shouts, skipping through the school gates like a little girl, twirling around with outstretched arms. 'Isn't it awesome?'

The sky opens up, gets bluer, brighter. The high, ivy-covered outer wall retreats behind a thick curtain of swaying trees and disappears as the grass verge widens and makes space for us. Across the road, the dense trees of Crowham Wood look as menacing as ever, but on *our* side of road thick clusters of purple Michaelmas daisies sway gracefully in the breeze.

The air smells clearer, too – crisp and tingling with excitement – now that it's Saturday and we're free to do what we please. And best of all, all the weird stuff that's happened since the start of term is forgotten – the freaky visions and fainting spells, the weird teachers, the bad dreams.

It *is* awesome!

The footpath rounds a corner and Crowham village comes into view, like a toy town nestled in a narrow river valley between two green, bare-sided hills. I can make out the high pitched roofs with their shiny slate tiles, the old church with the stubby square steeple, a little splodge of village green.

'I saw You-Know-Who in the quad yesterday,' Hannah says. 'Did I tell you?'

You-Know-Who. *Boom.*

Two weeks have gone by since Caleb arrived, and things have been getting back to normal – no more bad dreams or funny turns for me. No more tears or panic attacks or collapsing for Jordan, either. He's made friends with Darshan, another new Year 3 boy who cried so hard on the first day of term. Jordan seems less anxious, too – maybe the *fings* have gone away. Maybe they were never actually here.

As for me, I've spent the past weeks *not* looking at Caleb, *not* saying his name out loud, not thinking about his face or what happened – no, what I *thought* happened – on the night he arrived. He's just a boy, I tell myself – an ordinary boy who's got nothing whatsoever to do with me.

Hannah's been keeping tabs on him, though, and now I'm worried. *I saw him the quad.* Does she mean saw him from afar, or saw him and hung out with him? I can't believe how ridiculous I feel – my stomach's all fluttery, like I'm going to be a bit sick.

The fact is Hannah would be a perfect match for someone

like Caleb. She's pretty and petite, like a Beyoncé mini-me, with huge brown eyes, masses of curly black hair that she usually keeps tied back or plaited, and smooth, spot-free skin. She doesn't dress up much, just jeans and a vest top under a cardigan or shirt, but she always adds something perfect, like what she has on today – a flowery silk scarf and a blue sequinned beret.

'And?' Somehow, I manage to swallow the glob of jealousy that's built up in the back of my throat.

'*And* he was talking to Nat Ashmore,' Hannah grumbles, kicking a stone along the pavement. 'Typical, eh? Why do the hot ones always go for girls like her?'

'Well, it's not for her brains,' I sigh, hating myself for the relief I feel.

Hannah and I come to a junction and get ready to cross on to the B-road that runs through Crowham village. I glance to the right and left. The road's empty so I hurry across, but Hannah stays behind. There's no traffic, but she takes ages to cross, looking back and forth, right and left, again and again.

'Sorry,' she says as she catches me up. 'My parents are missionaries. I'm used to living in places where life is cheap. I'm a bit over-cautious, I guess.'

I look at her and raise my eyes.

50

'All right, Maddy,' she laughs. 'Paranoid, then. But if you'd seen the things I have – human road-kill, yeah? – you'd be paranoid, too.'

'So where are your parents now?'

'Rwanda. Mum's setting up an immunisation clinic there; Dad's training social workers.'

'I thought they were missionaries.'

'They are,' Hannah says. 'By serving others they are serving God.'

'And you're not from South Africa?'

'I've lived all over the place. My last school was in Cape Town, but it's not really home. Nowhere is. Mum's from Lesotho originally. She and Dad got together when they were both students in Brighton. Maybe that's the reason they picked Crowham. It's close to where they met.'

She doesn't say any more about her family, and she doesn't ask about mine. I already told her I don't have a dad. I mean, I do – everybody does. It's just that mine's never mentioned. He walked out when I was a baby, so what's there to say?

We spend the rest of the walk arguing about what *really* matters – whether or not Nat Ashmore's pair of prize-winning bazoombas are real or just an early present from Father Christmas.

In a few minutes we're on the village high street. Narrow

buildings tower over us, with dark slate roofs and tall chimneys like wonky top hats. At ground level are the shops – a newsagent's, a teashop, a pub. A tiny florist's window is crammed with autumn bouquets and Halloween displays.

Hannah looks up at the rooftops and squints. 'Remember what I said about the school being creepy?' She shivers, and tugs at the edges of her cardigan. 'Well, this place is worse – don't you think?'

I look around. There are cobblestoned alleyways with flint-tiled walls, flower boxes in the windows, cats purring on doorsteps.

'It's cute,' I say. 'Isn't it?'

'Look closer at the buildings. Those markings – can't you see?'

All the houses and shops in the village are hundreds of years old. They're made of wood and rough plaster and silver-blue flint.

'The windows,' Hannah whispers.

Finally, I see what she's talking about. Around every window, there are deep marks, thick slashes cut into the wooden frames or into the mortar that holds the windows in place. It looks like a huge animal – a wolf or a bear – has tried to claw its way into the houses . . .

'Still think Crowham village is cute?'

I run my hand along a window ledge. There are other marks, too – faint circles etched around the slashes.

'Well, it's not cute,' Hannah says, shuddering again. 'Or even quaint. It's just weird, plain and simple.'

We split up as soon as we get to the market square. Hannah's got errands to run and I want to send a message to Mum. There's decent wi-fi at Crowham's branch of the county library, so I wave goodbye to Hannah and watch her disappear into the chemist's. I follow the pavement past the café's steamed window and peek over St Michael's church's stone and flint wall.

Through the jungle of overgrown grass and wilting flowers I can make out the tilting, narrow slabs that mark the ancient graves in the churchyard. A sliver of ghost hovers over one of them, silently swooshing in the gentle breeze, still lost, still waiting – for what?

It's just weird, Hannah said. What if she knew what I could see – what would she think then?

The library's on the other side of the road so I press the button at the zebra crossing and wait for the light to change. I look back at the church. Something flickers in the corner of my eye – a dim light through one of the clear, leaded windows, like a tarnished mirror reflecting the sun. The green crossing man blinks and shrieks at me to go, but I can't move. It's definitely

53

there, in the window – a weird greyish smudge, like the one I saw in the window on the first day of term and the next day, in my mirror, when Jordan told me about the *fings*.

Traffic trundles by – a tractor pulling some kind of plough, a local charity's minibus, a dirty white van. I press the button again and look back. There's nothing in the window – no dark light – but I see a tall human shape standing in the graveyard, facing the church, looking up at the glass . . .

The light's about to change to red so I step into the road, still looking behind me.

I hear it first – the horrible screech of tyres, the frantic blast of a horn.

Then I feel it – not the thud of hard metal against my smashable bones, not the painful impact I'm expecting, but something soft, airy – a cold pillow of whoosh that sweeps between the car and me just as I should have been hit.

The car jack-knifes to the left, its back end swerving on to the other side of the road. A car going the opposite direction slams on its brakes, skids to halt. I stumble forward – *what just happened?* – until I lose my balance and sprawl hands-first on to the ground.

In an instant, the driver of the jack-knifing car opens her door and climbs out.

'Omigod, I *hit* someone,' she screams. She's looming over me, a blurred denim monster, waving her arms to attract attention. 'Please, anyone, help us, *please.*'

'It's okay,' I whisper.

I roll on to my side. Nothing hurts. My hands sting from where I tried to break my fall, but that's all.

I push myself on to my knees and slowly stand up.

'Oh my God.' The woman backs away, a terrified look on her face.

'It's okay.' I brush my burning palms on the sides of my jeans. My voice is calm, slow. 'You didn't hit me.'

'Well, I hit bloody something,' the woman squawks. She points at the bonnet of her car to show me the evidence, but nothing's damaged. The shiny paintwork isn't even scratched.

'But I felt it,' she says. 'Right here.' She bends over and takes a closer look, touching the smooth, undented surface. 'I know I did.' She backs towards the car, looking at me suspiciously. Does she think I'm playing a trick on her? Her face reddens with anger, as if she's annoyed that I'm not face down on the road, dying.

'The light had gone green,' she spits. 'You just stepped into the road . . .'

The driver of the other car pulls away. The people watching from the pavement move on, too. There's no blood on the ground, no ambulance on the way – it's a bit of a bore, actually.

I watch them all saunter back to their cars, or nip into shops.

I look towards the church. There's no one lurking in the graveyard – I must have imagined it – just the usual oblivious ghosts.

'I felt it,' the lady says, getting into her car, still dazed. 'I definitely felt *something*.'

By the time I get to the library I've finally stopped shaking. *Just weird*, Hannah said. *Plain and simple*.

I find a desk next to a huge window that looks over a little play park. I log in to a computer. Outside, a five-year-old boy is digging in the sandbox with a red bucket and blue spade. He flings sand into the air and the little girl playing beside him gets some in her eye and starts to wail. In a second the girl's mum is beside them, whisking her daughter to safety, brushing the sand from her eyelashes, smoothing her hair.

When I go online, Mum's waiting for me. It's the middle of the night in LA, but sometimes, like today, I catch her awake, and we can have a proper chat. I tell her about Hannah, about how I feel like I've known her a long time, even though it's only been a few weeks.

It takes her a few minutes to reply.

That's great, she says. *Just be careful*.

Careful? Of what?

She's lovely, Mum. Really.

I'm sure she is. Mum sends the message and then starts typing again. *But it doesn't pay to get too close to people, does it?*

I look at the words and sigh. What's her *problem*?

More typing. *It's just that I don't want you to get hurt, darling. Remember those other girls?*

Why does she always have to remind me? She must know how lonely I am – doesn't she want me to have friends?

But Hannah's really kind, I write. *And her parents move around a lot, so she's not likely to just up and leave in the middle of term like Olga or Severine.*

Mum ignores me. *Anybody else new this year?*

I think about Caleb.

No nice boys? She types in a little wink symbol. I hear the rumble of imaginary thunder – it's like she *knows*.

Yuck. I send a sick face sticker. *Don't be disgusting.*

We talk about other stuff – the storms that have been battering the West Coast, the winds that shake the windows so hard that she thinks it's an earthquake. For my part, I don't tell Mum about what happened with the car. I don't mention the ghosts, either, of course – I'm not allowed. I wish I could tell her – I so desperately want to – but I don't breathe a word about the nightmares or visions or Jordan's *fings*.

What would be the point? She'd only worry, like I'm

worrying about LA – those stupid storms, the dreaded word 'earthquake'. And what could she do from California? This far away from each other, it's best not to tell.

On the way home, Hannah notices how quiet I am.

'I'm okay,' I tell her. 'It's just, well, I kind of got hit by a car.'

'Oh my goodness, Maddy!' She puts her hand up to her mouth, shocked. 'What happened?'

'Nothing, really. I'm all right, but it was, well . . . weird.'

'Weird? What do you mean?'

Here's my chance to tell her, but what would I say?

Weird, as in something stopped the car from actually touching me.

And she'd say, *Like an air bag?*

And I'd go, *Yeah, exactly like an airbag, only invisible.*

And she'd be like, *Whoa, that's cool. What was it?*

And then I'd say, *I'm not sure, but it could have something to do with these ghosts I've been able to see for most of my life.*

She'd go, *Ghosts, that's so awesome, Maddy.*

And I'd be all –

'Maddy?'

I sigh, shrug, kick a stone along the pavement. I think about what Mum said – *just be careful.*

'Like I said, it was weird. Scary and weird.'

It's nearly dark. We walk faster – there are no street lights once we're off the main road. The trees of Crowham Wood and the walls surrounding the school take on lives of their own – branches grow like arms, ivy spreads and stretches like quivering tentacles. Hannah and I don't say anything else, and the silence feels like a gaping hole – I want to fill it up with words, explanations, stories – tell her all the things I know I never can.

The huge iron school gate squeaks as we push it open and shut it again – imprisoning ourselves. We trudge up the gravel path in silence. I can see the school's lights come on, flickering through the windows so the front of the building looks like the angry face on a Halloween pumpkin.

'Well,' Hannah says softly, 'we made it home.'

Home, I think. And for the first time since I left Mum behind at LAX, since I walked through the security gates all on my own and didn't once look back, since I got on the plane and clung to the arms of the seats during take-off because I didn't have Mum's hand to hold, since I walked up the path to the Crowham Martyrs school and thought I was going to be pushed away by the throbbing knot of ghosts that were waiting for me at the top of the drive, I want to break down and cry.

While Hannah opens the door, I check the nearest windows for those slash marks – none here, whatever that means.

The entrance hall is empty, except for the scowling prefect who watches us sign ourselves in – there's no one to ask us how our day has been, nobody to wonder if we're hungry or offer to make us nice cups of tea. There's a roaring fire in the hearth – that explains the flickering light – but it doesn't look at all cosy. As I gaze into the flames I see burning figures, funeral pyres collapsing into piles of embers and ash.

'Come on,' Hannah says. 'You've had a shock.'

Our feet glide along the polished marble floor as she leads me across. We climb up the stairs to the mezzanine. Down one of the narrow corridors someone must be watching TV – I hear a shrill advert, then the *Hollyoaks* theme. Creeping along in the dim light reminds me of Caleb, and the night he arrived. Normally, that memory would make me smile, make my heart beat a little faster, make me let out an involuntary sigh. Now, I do nothing – feel nothing. What happened that night's just another bizarre occurrence in a term that's already overcrowded with them.

'Shall we have a hot chocolate?' Hannah asks. 'I've got a jar of instant in the back of my cupboard.'

'Sorry,' I say. 'I need to do some reading for Monday.'

Her face falls – it's a lame excuse, a brush-off, anybody could see that. But I don't want to talk any more. I just want to think. What should I do about all this weird stuff that's going on? Where can I go? Who could I tell?

The answers are already in my head, of course. Nothing. Nowhere. Nobody.

Like that promise to Mum – *never, ever.*

Hannah's room is on the second floor, just down from my attic steps. She stops at her door and reaches out, touching my shoulder.

She gives me a quick air kiss. 'You sure you're all right, Mads?'

I nod. 'I'm fine. Really.'

Her mouth twists up on one side – she knows I'm not.

'You can talk to me, you know? Whatever's going on, well . . . I think I'd understand.'

Tears sting my eyes. It hurts, not being able to say anything, not daring to tell my one and only friend the truth about . . .

Hannah opens the door. In a second she's vanished, like one of the ghosts.

11

'Sir, Jake farted again.'

Hannah looks up at me from across the table and shakes her head.

'It wasn't me, Sir,' Jake whines. 'Honest.'

On the other side of the assembly hall, Mr Casey shields Jake from an attacking gang of spray-deodorant-wielding Year 7s.

'Whose idea was this anyway?' Hannah mutters jokingly, picking up a fat felt-tip pen.

'It was yours.'

We've been at this an hour – cutting tongue-shaped flames from patterns traced by Jordan and Darshan on sheets of red and orange card. They're going to be used on the Crowham Martyrs School float in the Bonfire Night parade. Jake and the other Year 8 boys are cutting pieces of heavy card meant to look like torches.

Hannah press-ganged me into this pointless exercise after

she came back from church in the morning. Divine inspiration or something.

'Come on,' she'd said, dragging me from my cosy bed. 'It'll take your mind off what happened in town yesterday.'

'Nothing happened –'

'With the car, I mean.'

I crawled back on to my bed, pulled the duvet over my head.

'Oh, come on, Maddy – it'll be fun.'

It's not. My hands ache from using the industrial-sized scissors, but Hannah's humming to herself as she works, and her face shines with contentment, as if she's got some sort of inner light. I know it's wrong, but I envy her. Okay, so she thinks Crowham's a creepy place, but she's obviously got no ghosts to cloud her vision of life, no *fings* to make her wonder what's real and what's not real. Otherwise, how could she be so happy?

There are others in the room, of course – and I don't just mean the ghosts that weave in and out through the narrow stained-glass windows like children playing It.

Nat Ashmore and Caleb – they must a proper couple now – are talking to Mr Casey, strolling around the room, surveying the workers. Natalie walks tall and straight-backed as she heads towards us, as if she's already been named the Bonfire Queen and is balancing an imaginary crown on her head. Caleb and

Mr Casey follow in her wake like loyal servants, Mr Casey humming the tune to *Remember, remember . . .*

'Hello, ladies.' Nat picks up one of the flames that I've cut out, inspecting it.

I scowl at her but Hannah – perfect Hannah – smiles, of course.

'This is going to be an amazing float,' Hannah trills. 'I *love* the design.'

'I hope we can get the fire effect to work on the night,' Nat says. She turns to Caleb, giggling and batting her eyelashes. 'But I suppose that's up to my men.'

I look at Caleb, fighting the urge to roll my eyes, and see the corner of his mouth turn up. He glances down at me and for a second I feel that connection again. His smile spreads across his face, lighting it up.

And then I hear something – flames? Is this a sound effect for the float? The sound is tinny and muted, like it's playing through somebody's headphones.

Mr Casey bends over our table, sketches out a diagram of the float, and I can hear his explanation of how the fire machine will work. 'We've got to make sure we get the chemistry right – don't want to blow up the entire village.'

The crackling sound gets louder. I look around – where's the person listening to the music?

A woman screams. Only it's not anyone in the room, or even in the school, it's just a sound in my –

I shake my head. No. I won't let it happen again. I won't get all weird here, not in front of –

The noises get louder, more distinct – an angry shout, a creaking chain – but I can still make out what people in the assembly hall are saying, so if I hang on long enough, maybe this feeling will pass, like a storm.

But no . . . no. The fire sound is deafening, roaring over the weeping and wailing and groaning and grinding. I put down my scissors, pull my chair in closer, grab a table leg with one of my hands, so I can stay upright.

'Isn't that right, Maddy?'

Someone's talking to me. I scan the faces, but they're all a blur, one indistinct line of pulsating skin. I force my mouth into a smile, try to focus my eyes, tune in my hearing.

No use. My stomach churns as the grinding gets louder and the screams pierce the muffled ether of background noise. I look up. Where are the playful ghosts? That pretty one? I need to focus on something familiar even if it's only –

There's a spot of something grey and dark on the ceiling. *Fings*, I think. Bad things – worse than the wave of ghosts that is swooshing towards me, thickening into a wall of white . . .

My stomach heaves.

I manage to get out of the chair and stagger towards the other side of the room. There'll be something there for me to throw up in, somewhere I can –

A narrow strip of sunlight cuts through a gap between two thick black curtains.

I blink to adjust my eyes. Wherever I am, it stinks. Musty and damp like old, rotten wood. My hip bones ache, so I can't be anywhere that's soft or comfy.

I'm lying on a cold, hard floor surrounded by stacks of wooden chairs, whose legs enclose me like the bars of a makeshift prison. I cough a couple times, then sneeze out some dust. As I sit up, I feel moisture seeping through my clothes and on to my skin. I haven't wet myself, have I?

No. It's something else – I can smell it. Sick. All over my top.

'Maddy?'

A man's voice. For a moment I panic, thinking of my dreams, being dragged along the clifftop – but it's only Mr Casey.

'Where am I?' As I struggle to stand, Mr Casey goes to the curtains, pulling them back another inch or two so that I can see.

'The storeroom behind the stage. You had another blackout.'

'Where are the others?'

'What *others*?' He closes the curtains again, looks around anxiously. 'Who do you mean?'

'I don't know. Hannah. Jordan and Darshan – everybody who was working on the float.'

'They're still in the assembly hall,' he whispers. 'But we needed to get you away from them.'

'I'm better now, Sir. And I don't think I'm contagious.'

I step towards the curtain, closer to the narrow band of light. I don't want to be standing in the darkness with Mr Casey – what if somebody finds us in here?

'I need to get back to my room,' I say.

Mr Casey shakes his head. 'It's safer here. For now.'

'I'm fine,' I croak. My heart is fluttering and another wave of sickness pushes up towards my throat. Why is Mr Casey being so weird?

'That's not what I mean.'

I want to ask him what he *does* mean but I don't dare open my mouth.

He whispers the words, 'I *know*, Maddy.'

A subtle swoosh of the curtains. A silent *boom* in my ears.

'I know who you are.'

I swallow to keep the sick down. What is he talking about – has he gone mad?

'And I can't let you get into any sort of trouble.'

'But, I haven't done anything wrong, Sir.'

'I don't mean you,' he snaps. 'I mean with *him*, I mean . . .'

'Who are you talking about, Sir?'

Suddenly the air thickens with dust and musty fumes. I can hear Mr Casey breathing – a throaty rasp, then a fit of heavy coughing, as if every breath's a struggle, as if somebody has him by the throat and is choking out the air. I go to the curtain and pull it back. As the bright sunlight hits I'm afraid that he'll shout something from a vampire movie like, *It burns, it burns* but instead he digs in his trouser pockets, and pulls out an asthma inhaler, taking a massive puff.

'Mr Casey? Are you okay?'

'Fine,' he croaks.

He coughs and sputters until he regains his composure. He looks at me, then outside at the sunshine, then back towards the half-open door to the stage. His grey eyes flash with fear. His hands are shaking too, and his head twitches back and forth.

'I'm sorry,' he says.

'It's not your fault you're asthmatic.'

'I mean, for what I said about . . . ' He mouths the word, hardly making a sound. '*Him.*'

He coughs and twitches and takes another puff on the inhaler.

'Who is *him*, Sir?' I whisper. I look around – is someone else in the room with us? 'Do you mean the headmaster? Mr Grayling?'

'I mustn't say any more,' Mr Casey mutters. 'I must keep –'

He's trembling all over – has he been drinking? Has he got the shakes – is that what's wrong?

'I'm going back out, Sir.' I step backwards, towards the door.

'N-no. You mustn't.'

'I'll be all right. Really.'

I keep moving away.

'I mean it, Maddy,' he says. 'I *know* . . .'

When I step out on to the dark stage, Mr Casey's still talking, muttering randomly between wheezes and gasps. On the other side of the closed curtains I can hear the Bonfire Committee in the assembly hall, laughing and chatting. A pair of scissors clatters on to the floor and somebody shrieks.

I feel my jumper – still wet from where I got sick. I can't go out there, not looking like this – not smelling like –

'Maddy?' A deep voice from the opposite side of the stage.

I don't answer. My heart flutters in my throat.

'Is that you, Maddy? I can hardly see.'

Someone shuffles closer. I can only see an outline – long hair, broad shoulders –

'It's me, Maddy. Caleb.'

I sigh, and blink back tears of relief.

'Sorry,' I say, 'I thought . . .'

'Are you all right, Maddy? Everybody's worried – Miss Burke sent me to check.'

Caleb's close enough to see how dreadful I look, to smell the reek of puke on my clothes.

'I got sick all over my top,' I say. 'I wouldn't come any closer if I were you.'

He reaches out to touch my arm. As his hand gets closer to my skin, I feel something strange – a pulse of energy between us, a current. When he touches me, it's like a shock.

'Whoa – what was that?'

Caleb steps back and the strange feeling subsides.

'I don't know,' he says, shaking his hand. 'Must be static electricity from the curtains or something.'

'Well, I'm feeling bad enough without you trying to electrocute me, okay?'

'Sorry about . . . whatever that was.'

The noise from the assembly hall gets louder – tables are being moved, metal clinks together as scissors are thrown into cardboard boxes. Everybody's packing up, putting things away. I hear laughter, too – Nat Ashmore's high-pitched giggle. Is she the one who sent Caleb after me? Is this a practical joke? Something she can tease me about later?

'I'd better get back,' I say.

I walk away, towards the side door that leads to the corridor, so I can avoid the others – I'm not in the mood for their laughter, their stares, or even their pity.

'Are you sure you're okay, Maddy?'

'I'm sure.'

It's too dark for me to see Caleb, but I can feel him, even from this distance. The weird pulse is faint, but it's still there, like an invisible cord, holding us together.

On the other side of the stage curtains Natalie Ashmore squeals again, and the other Year 10 girls join in with a chorus of laughter. The sound brings me back to my senses and I shake my head, rolling my eyes at my own stupid thoughts.

An invisible cord? *Really, Maddy?*

I reach the door and fumble for the handle.

'Maddy?' It's Caleb again, calling from the dark stage. 'Don't be scared.'

I open the door with trembling hands and step into the light. My heart pounds. What does Caleb mean? What does he know?

Don't be scared of *what?*

12

'They should have taken you to a doctor.'

Hannah's sprawled across her bed, holding a book with one hand, twiddling the corner of the bedspread with the other, twisting and untwisting it.

'I'm fine,' I say. 'Mr Casey was in far worse shape than me – all that coughing and gasping. I never knew asthma could be like that.'

Hannah's room is like mine – a five-square-metres reminder of a far-away family, a distant home. Her bedspread is made of thin cotton, an orange and fuchsia batik. There are blown-up photographs that must have been taken on a safari holiday: lions resting beside a shaded pool, a flock of flamingos taking off against the sunset. There's a smaller picture of her parents' wedding. Her handsome dad's wearing a cream linen suit and leather sandals – he's the ultimate English gentleman, pale skin, a floppy fringe pushed back from his forehead. Her mum's wearing a traditional African wedding dress with matching headpiece, a high scarf embellished with intricate gold braid and silvery lace. Hannah looks more like her mum – deep dimples and a bright smile.

I look down at my laptop screen. I'm meant to be reading over the first few paragraphs of a geography project but the page goes blurry and I can't concentrate on the effects of climate change on the water cycle.

I know who you are.

Maybe Mr Casey was just ranting yesterday, all those crazy things he was saying. Maybe the asthma had cut off the oxygen to his brain, made him temporarily deranged.

I rub my eyes, stare out the window, watch bare trees sway against the grey sky.

When I look back at my homework, there's something on the screen besides geography, something written in bold font and underlined.

I know who you are.

How did those words get there? Did I type them? I shake my head – I must be more tired than I thought.

'What's the matter?' Hannah asks.

'Nothing.' I blink and rub my eyes. 'I'm going to need a break pretty soon, though.'

'I know something's wrong,' Hannah says. 'More than your eyes.'

'I'm fine,' I say. 'Just sleepy.'

I tap the keyboard, delete those random words.

'Why do you live in the attic room, Maddy?'

'What?'

'By yourself. Away from the others?'

'I don't know.'

'Well, who put you there?' Hannah's words are clipped – she sounds harsher, bossier, more like a teacher than a friend.

'Missy, I suppose,' I say. 'Miss Burke.'

'Why?'

'I don't know.' I put my hands up in exasperation. 'Why don't you ask her?'

'Sorry,' Hannah says, and her voice softens again. 'It just seems unfair. Stuck up there like a prisoner.'

'I don't mind. Really. I've always been happier on my own.'

She shakes her head. 'I don't believe you.' Hannah sighs, and goes back to her book. She makes a big show of it, flopping down on the bed, turning the pages loudly.

I try to carry on with my work, but my mind keeps going back to what Mr Casey said yesterday.

Him.

Maybe he meant Caleb. I remember that weird vibration

between us, that *don't be scared* – and suddenly my hands are shaking.

I know who you are.

I rest my fingers on the keyboard, nudge the screen so that Hannah won't see anything if she looks up from her books.

Because it's not just my hands that have gone wobbly. I feel something in my stomach, deep down, as if I've swallowed a huge, heavy stone and it's being turned over and over by an invisible hand.

I'm seeing things, too. Something's appearing on my laptop screen – letters and words, but I didn't type them.

Did I?

No, I couldn't have. They're old-fashioned letters that I can't even read.

A blink and rub my eyes. What's happening?

The screen flickers and the letters get darker and fatter, the words get clearer – *foul* something or other, *begot*. I put my hands down at my side, ball my hands into fists – but the words don't stop . . . *lamentable childe . . . mine own dear*

My teeth chatter as I try to stop my body from shaking. Why am I seeing things? Am I going mad?

an unholy prince

Quickly – close the lid, Maddy, hide the screen, make this stop.

I put my both hands on the lid, squeeze it as tightly as I can, but underneath I can still hear the keyboard.

Tap, tap, tap.

I look over at Hannah. She's gone back to her book, thank goodness.

I breathe in deeply, and let out a sigh, so she'll think I'm fed up of my homework.

Okay, Maddy. Now open the lid. Slowly. Those words will all be gone, you'll see.

The screen has dimmed to a dark grey. The words *are* gone, but now there's a picture – an old-fashioned black and white drawing like the ones Mr Casey showed in that history lesson.

It's blurred, like the words were, but I can make out tall trees. A huge fire. When I lean in closer, I see indistinct figures – people, I suppose, but they could be animals, they could be –

'Maddy?'

I sit up with a start and look back at the screen. Everything's gone, replaced by my homework.

'What's the matter, Mads?'

'Nothing,' I say, closing the laptop, pushing it away from me.

'You've gone all pale,' Hannah says. 'You look like you've seen a ghost.'

That almost makes me laugh – but no ghost could have done this, could they?

'Maddy, are you –'

'I'm not feeling very well,' I say, and suddenly that's true. I put my hand over my mouth, as whatever was resting in my belly seems ready to heave itself out.

'I think I'm going to be sick.'

In a flash, I'm up and out the door, racing down the narrow corridor to the bathroom.

I find an empty toilet cubicle, slam it shut, lock the door.

Just in time. I stand there, shivering and shaking, emptying my stomach until nothing more can come out and I feel halfway normal.

That's when I see it – a dark stain between my legs, blood seeping into the cloth of my jeans. In an instant, the feeling in my belly changes from a queasy sickness to a dull, deep pain.

So is that what this is all about? Those hallucinations?

I'm having my period.

I feel faint, dizzy. I'm having my *first* period.

I sort myself out as best I can. There's a pink fabric-covered 'sanitary box' that's full of what I need. When I'm finished I stand in front of the sink and look into the mirror. Do I look any different? A bit paler, I think. My face is puffier than normal. Will people be able to tell? Will everyone know?

Then one of the juniors comes in and I quickly slip back into the corridor. The coast is clear so I tiptoe back to Hannah's.

'I was just about to check up on you,' she says, opening the door to let me in.

'I'm fine,' I say, teeth chattering.

'Just . . .'

I pull a face.

'That time of the month?' she says.

I nod, and I can feel my throat tighten.

'Is this your first?' she asks.

Tears stream down my cheeks, and I can't help my face from totally collapsing.

Hannah puts her arms around me. 'It's okay,' she says. 'You'll be okay.'

'I won't,' I sob. I feel so pathetic. So weak, blubbing into Hannah's strong shoulders.

'Of course you will, Mads,' Hannah coos.

I close my eyes for a moment – so tired, I could drop off to sleep, leaning against Hannah. It's like I'm dreaming – I'm on that clifftop, looking up at the sky, down at the sea. Nobody else this time. Just me.

'Mummy?'

I look all around me, but all I see are grey, heavy clouds above a vast expanse of dry, brittle grass. All I hear is the sea's roaring thunder.

'Mummy, where are you?'

No answer. She's gone. Lost.

I'm all alone.

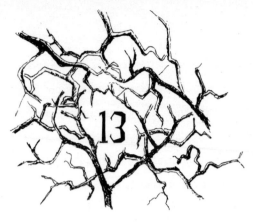

13

A week goes by – lessons, homework, assemblies – then another week, and another, and another, until it's nearly half-term and things are back to normal.

Normal for Crowham, anyway. Normal for me.

Mr Casey's his usual dishevelled self in history, wiping the backs of his hands on his crumpled brown trousers, and tugging at his hair. He never mentions what happened in the storeroom – the strange things he said, how frightened we both were. He's totally relaxed in lessons, as if it never happened, as if he doesn't remember.

The *fings* that tormented Jordan at the beginning of the term have disappeared, too – at least he doesn't seem afraid any more, and I haven't seen them. Maybe they were part of settling in – bizarre manifestations of Jordan's anxieties and fears. Now that he's mates with Darshan he seems happy and boisterous, a normal little boy.

And me?

I still see the ghosts, of course – it would be weirder if I *didn't* see them – but it's been weeks since I had a funny turn, and I don't hear those terrifying noises any more or have any nightmares, or see any strange pictures.

Maybe I'm like Jordan – maybe all I needed was someone like Hannah, a proper friend.

I've almost forgotten about Caleb, too. That 'connection' I felt the night he arrived, that weird shock when he touched me on the darkened stage. How stupid was I to think those things meant anything? When I pass him in the corridor I look at the floor, let my downcast eyes follow the dusty, grit-filled gaps between the polished boards. I'm embarrassed to think what I imagined about him – that we were linked somehow, that we knew each other.

It must have been hormones or something. That's the reason I heard those terrifying sounds, why I saw old-fashioned words jump out of computer screens, why I imagined people and places that don't exist.

It's a bit like Mr Casey and that asthma attack – who knew having your period could be so bad?

A seagull screeches over my head and swoops down to attack its prey – a half-eaten kebab that's fallen out of an overflowing bin.

It's warm for October, and the sun's shining brightly. Brighton's Lanes are packed with shoppers and day-trippers and kids on half-term like me. I'm sitting at an outside café table in Sussex Square, waiting for Hannah, who's rushed back to buy a dress she saw in a charity shop window and just *has* to have.

It's funky here – brightly lit shops selling candles and beads, hipster mums pushing toddlers wearing alpaca caps. It reminds of me Venice Beach, except not everyone's riding a skateboard or trying out yoga moves.

As I wait for the waiter to bring my hot chocolate, I notice something on the wall behind me. A faded, worn plaque – not a bright blue one that says somebody famous lived here, but a square slate with words etched into the eroded surface reads:

Margaret Cooper, on 12 April, 1675, was removed from her home on this site and taken to the village of Crowham where she was tried as a witch and hanged on 21 April of that same year.

My stomach does a flip. I hold my breath, listen for the rumble, the screams, the sounds of terror, but there's nothing except the seagulls screeching, the chatter of happy conversations, and the silent ghosts – thick as fog, cold as a mist rolling in off the sea. They swirl around the square, swooping like translucent starlings through the narrow passageways that link the square to the rest of the Lanes and the streets beyond.

'Maddy!'

The ghost fog thins as Hannah winds her way through the crowds. They seem to be flying away from her, creating a path for her to walk through.

She sits down and orders a coffee, a proper one without any frothy milk or chocolate sprinkles on the top. She ignores the waiter's flirtatiousness, and shows me the dress – vintage silk, pink and floaty with hand-stitched flowers all around the neck and hemline. Then she reaches into her handbag and takes out a jumper, shivering slightly.

I look up at the sky. It might be the thickening ghost cloud, but it definitely seems to be getting colder – darker, too. It's so gloomy that I can hardly see the man in top hat and tails who walks into the square, followed by a group of tourists.

'This is the most haunted part of what used to be Brighthelmstone village,' the man says. 'It's the oldest quarter of Brighton, full of ghostly lore that will make your spine tingle.'

A woman takes out a camera, photographs the tour guide

standing in front of the thin, darkening passage between buildings that's positively clogged with ghosts.

'Now in this pub, used as the village's jail during the eighteenth century, a ghost the locals call Old Jake has been terrifying landlords, cellar men and barmaids for hundreds of years.'

The guide doesn't know that Old Jake has got hundreds – probably thousands – of mates with him. They're thickening again, despite Hannah's presence. They hover around our table, annoyingly, so I push them away, like I'm swatting a fly.

'What?' Hannah says. She scrapes her chair along the cobblestones in a panic, before standing up. 'Was that a bee?'

'No,' I laugh.

She scans the air as if she doesn't believe me. 'Well, what was it, then?'

'What was *what*?'

'You.' She flutters both hands. 'Doing this.'

'Just a nervous tick,' I say. I try to laugh. She shakes her head, not entirely convinced.

'Seriously. It's nothing.'

But the ghosts are so dense here, a gauzy film turning people into shadows, veiling Hannah's face. It's freezing, too – not even Hannah's goodness can keep the dankness at bay. I'm sitting directly opposite her, but I'm cut off from everything around me, isolated on a cold, windswept, fog-bound island of the dead.

As she leans towards me I feel warmer.

'It's not nothing, I know it's not. Do you feel sick again?'

I laugh, but I'm shivering with the cold, and my skin goes clammy.

'You've got to tell me,' she says.

'Tell you what?'

She pulls back again and her metal chair scrapes along the cobblestone paving. 'Seriously, Maddy, you're starting to annoy me.'

'What are you on about?'

'This.' She waves her hands again, like I did to swoosh away the ghosts. Her face gets flushed-looking, sweaty. 'And acting like it's nothing – those fainting spells, that seizure.'

'It was my period.'

'Your period?' She howls with laughter. A mum and toddler at the next table look over us.

'Sorry,' Hannah mouths. 'Your period?' She whispers this time. 'You really have gone mad if you think a period can do those things. Didn't your mum tell you *anything*?'

My face reddens, with both shame and anger. I'm embarrassed by my ignorance, but how dare she bring Mum into this?

'Seriously, Maddy, you don't collapse, you don't get twitchy hands. A few stomach cramps usually, wanting to snap at people, nothing more.'

'Maybe I'm an extreme case.'

She rolls her eyes. 'You should go to the doctor.'

'I've already been to the medical room.'

'A proper doctor, I mean. Fat lot Matron knows.'

'I'm all right,' I say. 'There's nothing wrong with me. It's all part of –'

'What? Growing up?'

'No. Something else.'

'Well?'

She's got me so rattled I almost blurt out the truth. I close my eyes, try to calm down, but I'm getting sick of this. I'm so tired of the interrogations and the hectoring that I want to tell her the whole truth – promise or no promise – just to shut her up, once and for all.

I open my eyes. 'All right,' I say. 'When you look around, what do you see?'

'People,' she says.

'Okay, what else?'

She twists in her chair, craning her neck. 'Old-fashioned stone buildings that have been turned into cafés and shops.'

'And . . .'

'Outside tables, rubbish bins . . .'

'Keep going . . .'

She looks upwards. 'The sky. Clouds. Seagulls.'

'Right,' I say. 'I see all those things. But I see other stuff, too.'

Hannah looks at me, scrunching up her face as if to say, What is this girl *on*?

'So, do you, like, hallucinate?'

I think for second, before shaking my head. 'No, but I see things that you don't, that no one else can.'

Now it's her turn to go a bit pale. Can she guess what I'm talking about? Does she know? Unconsciously – at least, I think it's just instinct – she touches her throat and for the first time I see that she's wearing a delicate gold chain around her neck, with a tiny cross hanging from it.

'I'm not a vampire or anything,' I say.

'Well, what are you, then?' She smiles, making out like she's joking. She taps her cross gently, rubs it between her fingers.

'I can see . . .'

Suddenly I hear a voice shouting across the square. 'No! Don't!'

I turn around, expecting to see . . . who – Mum? Missy?

But it's just a mother shouting at her little boy, warning him not to wander off the pavement and into the road.

I look back at Hannah. She's smiling. That light that's

keeping away the ghosts seems to have been turned up higher. The tiny cross at her throat glitters and glows.

'Ghosts,' I say.

'Sorry?' she says.

Louder this time. *'I can see ghosts.'*

14

The words came out so smoothly, slipped from my throat as easily as breathing.

I can see ghosts.

And, for a split second, I felt dizzy with the freedom of telling someone – telling a *friend* – the truth about myself.

I see ghosts. I said it not once, but *twice*. How brave is that?

'Maddy?'

Hannah's words bring me back to reality.

'I can't hear you, Mads. What did you say?'

The ghost fog has thickened. Not only can I hardly see her through the haze, but somehow the ghosts have managed to stifle my words.

'It was nothing,' I say. 'Only joking.'

I push my chair back, scrape it along the pavement. 'We'd better leave now or we'll miss the Crowham train.'

When Hannah goes inside to pay the bill, I pull my cardigan

tighter around my shoulders to keep out the cold and try to remember the first time I saw these bloody ghosts. It must have started somewhere, right?

London, I think. A day out to the Tower of London with Mum and one of her friends. I told her friend's kid about the white twirly things that were filling up the moat, and he got mad at me, like I was trying to scare him.

Was that the first time? Or is the real reason I remember the Tower ghosts because there were so many of them. Just like our old apartment building in Los Angeles – that place was heaving with ghosts, too. Under the stairwells, in the storerooms, and out on the streets, lingering in the entrances to abandoned buildings, loitering in alleys.

Were there so many ghosts in these places because bad things happened? The Tower of London – that stands to reason, all those executions, the hundreds of prisoners rotting away in their cells. Maybe bad things happened at the Cherokee Avenue Apartments, too. Poor old Edwina, with her puffy, bruised looking 'face'. Maybe she'd been murdered!

Then there's Crowham – the martyrs. It was a convent once, according to the history of the school, and the nuns were considered heretics. They were taken away and burned at the stake – no wonder the place is totally infested. And Brighton – the woman who was dragged away and hanged.

There was another place, too.

It was somewhere along the coast highway, when Mum and I were driving up to San Francisco. We stopped for a picnic high above the rocks at Big Sur.

I close my eyes and try to remember. That bright blue sky, the perfect waves lapping the shore. The ghosts, piled high into towers, rising up from the rocky ground like huge mountains of candy floss.

Did I dream them?

Must have – it was a pretty spot in the middle of nowhere, not a big city like LA, or an old prison like the Tower of London. It was just sand, rocks and sea – a normal sunny day, just me and Mum, picking flowers and arranging them into a bouquet that we set on the edge of the cliff.

So nothing could have happened there to bring those ghosts, could it? Unless it was something bad from a long time ago – a shipwreck, or a terrible mutiny far out in the sea.

Hannah touches my shoulder and I jump, my mind still back in California with Mum and the ocean and those massive mounds of swirling ghosts.

Was it a dream?

'Come on, Maddy. If we don't make this train, we'll miss the last minibus back to school.'

I run after her, and between the narrow Lanes catch a glimpse of the darkening sea.

A shipwreck, I think, as black clouds thicken.

The ghosts of dead sailors – is that what they were?

15

The bus lurches away from the gravel shoulder, gears grinding, and quickly builds up speed. I chase it as far as I can, shouting at the top of my lungs. Hannah doesn't bother – she sits down on the bus shelter's bench, calmly watching the tail-lights disappear around a bend.

As I tromp back to the bus stop, she takes out her mobile. It's dark enough for the light on the phone to reflect off her skin. She punches some numbers, waits a few seconds and shakes her head. She stands up and steps away from the shelter, closer to the road.

'This place is pathetic,' she says. 'In a village in Lesotho you can get mobile reception, so why not here? Call this a First World country?'

She shoves the phone back into her bag. 'At least my battery's charged – we can use it as a torch for the walk home.'

'It'll take ages,' I groan. 'We'll never get back before they lock the front door.'

'We will if we cut through the woods.'

My heart nearly stops. '*What?*'

'Don't look so shocked,' Hannah laughs. 'People use the path all the time.'

'During the daytime maybe, if they're brave enough or stupid –'

She pulls at the sleeve of my cardigan. 'Come on, Maddy, there's nothing to be scared of. It's not even completely dark.'

'It's dark enough.'

She laughs at my fear. 'Dark enough for what?'

Hannah's light cuts a tiny circle out of the blackness. I hold on to her arm as we walk. I hear nothing but our footsteps – soft soles on hardened dirt.

'You okay, Mads?'

I try to say, 'Yes,' but all that comes out is a voiceless grunt.

Hannah keeps the narrow beam pointed at the path. I stay focused on my breathing, keeping it as smooth as I can – in, out, in, out. I think only of what's close to me, not what might be out there in the woods, waiting, watching. Of Hannah's light. Of her strong footsteps and tight grip, her steady breathing beside my shallow, panicky gulps.

When we've walked for about five minutes she stops. 'See?' she says. 'What did I tell you? A doddle, yeah?'

She's right, I think. Of course, she's right. Taking the long way round would have been stupid. And there is nothing here to be frightened of. Trees, that's it. Lots of them. Nothing else. *Nothing*.

She shines the light into my face. 'You're doing a good job.'

I can only nod. I wish she'd stop talking, even if it's only in a whisper. What's the point of risking it? Why tempt anyone or anything that might be out there? Why not be quiet *just in case*?

'Seriously, Maddy. Facing your fears and –'

A sound behind us – a low, menacing growl – cuts her off.

See? I want to scream. *What did I tell you?*

We scuttle forward, away from the sound. I trip up on a stone, and nearly tumble on to the hard ground. Hannah stops and holds out her arm so that I can keep my balance.

It's quiet again. All I can hear is Hannah's breathing and my heart banging against my ribcage . . .

'Now you've got *me* spooked,' Hannah says.

'Didn't you hear that?' I whisper.

'Hear what?' Hannah says, and we're off again, taking purposeful strides along the path until, behind us, something rustles in the undergrowth and lets out another growl.

'That,' I rasp.

Hannah gulps, tensing her body, steeling herself. She turns around and with trembling hands, shines the torch on the path.

'Nothing's there,' she says, her voice tight.

The rustling gets closer. We back up, facing the sound, moving slowly away from it, both of us resisting the temptation to turn around and run for our lives.

Another growl. I grab Hannah's arm as something steps into the dim, quivering pool of light.

Eyes, like a cat's.

But cats don't growl this loudly or ferociously, not unless they're wild and huge like a puma or a cougar or a –

Those markings in Crowham village! The slashes on the windows – like massive claws. What were they? What kind of creature –

Something bounds towards us. Huge. Dark.

Fast.

Hannah lets out a groan. As her hand drops to her side, I reach for the phone and shine its light on the thing that's rapidly approaching.

A dog. That's all it is. I want to cry with relief. Just a dog! Not even a scary dog like an Alsatian or a Bulldog, but a clumsy, happy-faced black Labrador, with soft, harmless paws.

The growling has stopped, and the dog's barking excitedly. It scampers up to us and nearly knocks me over before backing down and rudely sniffing my clothes, tickling me, making me laugh.

'It's okay,' I say. The dog licks my face while I rub his floppy ears. 'He's harmless.'

Hannah takes a step away from it. She stands completely still and grabs the torch from my hand, clutching it tightly.

'I don't know, Mads.'

The dog stops barking and panting. He backs away, giving us space, leaving us alone.

'See?' I say. 'He's a good doggy.'

Hannah shakes her head, looks straight at the dog as if she doesn't dare take her eyes off him. 'We have to go.'

'Bye, bye, pooch,' I say, but the dog isn't paying attention to me any more. He's looking into the woods, his ears pricked, his head twitching. He opens his mouth, as if to bark, but no sound comes out, and then suddenly –

'Come on, Mads,' Hannah says. 'Let's go.'

The dog's whole body is shaking. His mouth opens and a foamy stream of saliva drops to the ground.

'Something's wrong with him,' I say.

'Exactly, Maddy. We need to go.'

Finally, the dog makes a noise. It's not a growl – it's that deep, husky, almost human moan we'd heard earlier.

'Now,' Hannah snaps. 'Hurry.'

She turns around, aims her light on to the path and walks away without looking back, taking long, steady strides.

'But the dog might be ill,' I say, trotting behind her.

'Shut up about that dog.'

'But he's –'

'It's not what you think.' Her voice sounds almost like the dog's – a throaty, bark.

She takes off running and I stumble after her, following the sound of her footsteps and the dim glow of her phone. After a few minutes she stops, lets me catch up. 'I've heard dogs like that in Africa,' she pants. 'I've seen them.'

I turn around, peer into the dark forest. 'You think it's got rabies?'

Hannah tugs at my arm, pulls me along the path.

'Hey,' I say. 'You're hurting me.'

'You think that's painful, Maddy?'

Her voice is a bark again. Angry. Bitter.

'You know nothing.'

16

'I heard what you said, Maddy.'

Hannah's voice is back to normal – warm, relaxed. Neither of us has said a word since we saw the dog in the forest. Has she forgotten about what happened now that we're back inside the school gates, crunching noisily up the gravel path?

'About the dog you mean?'

'What you said in Brighton. About seeing ghosts.'

I stop walking. Hannah does, too.

It's so quiet now, and my breathing's stopped, like I've been punched in the stomach.

Hannah heard me. I hunker over, covering my head with my arms in case something bad happens. In case a window breaks and showers me with shards of broken glass, or a tile flies off the roof, smashing my skull.

Hannah knows about the ghosts.

I stagger up the pathway, dazed and dizzy.

I told her.

Hannah opens the door and leads me into the hall. She scribbles our names into the sign-in book and makes sure the door's properly closed.

I watch a knot of ghosts flit near the fire, like tiny dancers.

'Can you see them, too?' I whisper, afraid to speak any louder.

'No,' she says, shaking her head.

She looks around the entrance hall, taking it all in – the glowing embers in the fireplace, the stained-glass windows, dull and smudgy looking without any light, the stairs that lead to darkness and gloom.

'But I can sense something,' she says, narrowing her eyes at me. 'It was in the woods tonight. I knew it would be, that's why I wanted to check it out. It's here, in the school, too.'

'What is it?'

She takes my arm, clutching it like she did in the woods, so tightly that it hurts. She leans in, whispers in my ear.

'*Badness.*'

We're drinking sweet, milky tea. Hannah's on her bed, legs curled up underneath her. I put my mug on the floor and sit down on a beanbag, stretching out, finally able to relax.

'You shouldn't sit there,' Hannah says. 'Not after what we saw in the woods. It might not be safe.'

'What do you mean?'

'Toko could –'

'What?'

'Tokoloshe –'

'Who?'

'That dog.'

I laugh nervously. 'He had a name?'

'If you knew the stories you wouldn't treat it like a joke.' She hops off her bed and tugs at my arm. 'Toko could grab your legs and pull you away.'

'All right,' I say, pushing myself to standing.

Hannah clears a space on the bed, so that I can sit beside her. 'Now,' she says, 'tell me about the ghosts.'

I shake my head. 'I can't.'

'What do you mean *can't?*' She looks at me sternly – and sounds like a teacher again, or a crabby old aunt.

'My mother told me never to talk about them – and I've already said too much.'

'Well, I'm afraid your mother doesn't understand.'

My cheeks burn. 'Understand what?'

'The bad power that is all around you.'

'The ghosts don't have any power. They're not bad. They're just annoying.'

'They are here for a reason – you must know that.'

Hannah's accent has changed, too. She's losing the posh English father, gaining the African mother.

'Did you not ask your mother why you see them?'

'I never asked her anything. I swore that I wouldn't.'

'Did you never ask *yourself*?'

'I used to,' I say.

'And now?'

I shrug. 'Now I'm not sure that I want to know the answer.'

She shakes her head and rolls her eyes, tutting at my foolishness.

'Your ghosts are connected to what I can sense – the *badness* – I'm sure of it. That day in history, during Mr Casey's lesson? Something was in the room. You know it as well as I do. And the morning Jordan collapsed, too. Not a virus like Miss Burke said. Not what you call annoying ghosts. Something worse. Something evil.'

'But the ghosts aren't evil –'

'I said they were *connected* to the *badness* – don't you listen? Maybe they're protecting you from it, like guardian angels. Did you never think of that? '

Hannah coughs. When she takes in a breath, her throat sounds wheezy, congested.

'What's the matter?'

She whispers, gasps. 'They think they can shut me up, but I'm too strong.' It sounds like she's choking, struggling to breathe. She waves her hands at a blue painted bureau.

'Top drawer,' she croaks.

I jump off the bed, tear across the floor, pull the top drawer open and dig through her things until I find a blue plastic asthma inhaler. By the time I hand it to her, her face is red and her breath comes out in tiny puffs.

She pumps the inhaler, takes in a massive gulp, holding it in for as long as she can before letting out the air and coughing again. When she fills her lungs a second time, her chest sounds clearer, her throat less constricted.

'That's better,' she says.

'This *badness*,' I whisper. 'What does it . . . look like?'

Hannah shakes her head. 'Not here,' she coughs. She pulls in closer to me. 'They can hear us.'

'Who can?'

She looks around the room, puts her fingers to her lips, motions for me to get up, and goes to the door.

'Follow me,' she whispers. 'I've got something to show you.'

Along the senior girls' corridor there's music – almost imperceptible, somebody has their speakers turned down low – coming from behind a bedroom door. There are no lights on, though. All the girls are tucked in – or would have been if their parents hadn't dumped them here – and fast asleep.

Hannah tiptoes dramatically, hopping from foot to foot in huge, exaggerated steps, like a pantomime explorer. When we get to the mezzanine, she steps in front of me, forcing me to stop.

'Where are we going?' I ask.

She crosses the mezzanine to the corridor where the medical room is. Matron's not on duty tonight, so the sickroom is locked. The rest of the black, endless corridor looms in front of us.

'Remember the day I visited you after you fainted?'

I nod.

'That's when I found it.'

'Found what?'

She puts a finger to her lips. 'Shhh!'

We stumble past the *No students beyond this point* sign and I listen out for the horrible growling I heard the night of Hannah's visit.

'Hurry, Maddy – we haven't got much time.'

She takes my hand and drags me along the corridor until we reach a closed, unmarked door. I must have seen it before – I know every Crowham cupboard, every tucked away storeroom, don't I?

Hannah opens the door, steps through. 'This way.'

She takes out her phone, flicks on the torch, tinting the space in front of us to a harsh greyish blue.

'Where are we?' I ask.

'You'll see.'

It's another corridor, even darker and narrower than the one we left behind, with a ceiling that seems to get lower with each step we take. Hannah holds out her phone, pointing it at the thick pipes that run along the top right corner, at the peeling, bubbling paintwork on the damp walls, at the grubby carpet that's daubed with dark, ominous stains.

'I don't like it here, Hannah.'

'Shhh,' she whispers. 'Stop being such a baby.'

Hannah opens a door that leads to the kitchen's back stairs, and another one that's just a cupboard full of mops and brooms and cleaning products.

'Can't we go back now?' I whine.

'Must be the next one.'

My heart is beating wildly, and my skin feels clammy, as if I'm about to faint again. The pipes clank, loudly, and I jump in fright.

'The boiler's come on,' Hannah laughs. 'You're not scared of central heating, I hope.'

The pipes clank again. They make a gentler sound this time – regular and rhythmic, like a signal – tap, tap, tap.

Hannah stands in front of another door. 'This is it,' she whispers. 'Are you ready?'

She turns the handle and steps inside. When I look into the blackness of the open doorway, I see nothing – not even the dull glow of Hannah's torch. But I feel a presence – is it something evil, or is it just the fear, clawing at my heart? It's inside the room, and outside, here on the threshold, surrounding me, making it hard to breathe, squeezing my chest, only this time there are no ghosts to help me – there's no softness to cushion falls or muffle sounds.

And at the other end of the corridor, something is waiting, too. I feel it on my skin, I know it –

The door squeaks open.

'Are you coming in or what?'

Hannah pulls me inside. She closes the door and flashes her light across the room.

It's full of bookcases, sagging under the weight of thousands of leather-bound volumes. It's a library of some sort, a storeroom for –

Outside, the pipes clank again.

'Listen,' Hannah whispers.

'I know. I heard.'

'No – something else.'

Further down the corridor, a door opens and closes. Footsteps pad towards us. Someone coughs – scratchy and rough.

'Mrs Gibson's room is on this floor.'

Another cough, just outside the door. That unmistakable rasp – it must be Mrs Gibson. Maybe she was what I sensed out in the corridor. Maybe she was who I heard the night I was in the medical room.

No, I tell myself. Mrs Gibson is just a cook. She's gruff and crabby, but she can't be *bad* – she can't be a *fing*.

Hannah turns the torch off as we flatten ourselves against the wall.

Mrs Gibson clears her throat – enough to let us know she's there – and opens the library door. I hold my breath, suck in my tummy, squeeze my eyes shut, as if doing these things will make me invisible.

The cool skin of Hannah's arm brushes against mine. She's not trembling or gasping for breath – how does she stay so calm?

Mrs Gibson lets out a little grunt and shuts the door. Her footsteps plod back down the corridor.

'Do you think she saw us?'

'I doubt it,' Hannah says, casually. 'She would have said something, wouldn't she? Would have chased us away?'

She flicks the torch back on, and steps towards a table in the middle of the room. Old leather-covered books are piled in awkward towers that look like they'll topple if we so much as breathe on them. Hannah leans in for a closer look, motions for me to join her.

'Weird, eh?' she says.

The titles on the spines are embossed in gold, but there are no authors named on any of these books, no publishers, no dates.

'Is that Latin?' Hannah asks.

'I don't think so.'

'What language is it, then?'

I shake my head. 'Come on. We shouldn't be here, especially since Mrs Gibson must have heard us.'

'No, Maddy. We have to show them.'

'What?'

'We have to show them we're not afraid.'

'But I *am* afraid. I'm bloody terrified. Please – let's go down to the kitchen or back to –'

'What exactly are you scared of?'

Hannah steps over to the one of the bookcases. She runs her fingers along the spines, raising dust that makes her sneeze.

'Books?'

'No.'

'Words on paper?'

'Of course not.'

'You're not afraid of Mrs Gibson are you? The head cook?'

Yes, I think. I am afraid of her. She can't be just a cook if she's in charge of these weird books, can she? And right now I'm scared of almost everyone at Crowham. And what Mr Casey said.

He. Him. Whoever that is.

Hannah touches the books again. 'Some of these don't even have titles – only symbols.'

I don't dare answer her. I'm waiting for something terrible to happen. A bookcase to come crashing down on top of us, the floor to collapse, the ceiling to cave in, burying us alive under tons of rubble or choking us with dust.

'Let's take some back to our rooms.'

She selects three books from the highest shelf and hands them to me, taking an armful for herself from a lower shelf.

'We shouldn't be doing this, Hannah . . .'

She tuts at my whinging, and tiptoes to the door. We go back the way we came, hurrying past the closed doors. By the time we get to her room, my arms ache with the weight of the books, and all I want to do is hide the stupid things until I can muster up the courage to take them back again.

'It isn't stealing,' she says, 'if that's what you're worried about. We haven't taken them from the school, we're borrowing –'

'I'm not worried about the books. I just didn't like it in there. All this stuff about toko-whosit and *badness* has –'

'Let's not talk any more.' Hannah puts her finger to her lips, and looks up and down the corridor. 'Tomorrow, when I get back from church, I'll tell you everything I know.'

'Tell me now,' I say. '*Please.*'

She leans closer to me, her lips almost touching my ear.

'It will be safer tomorrow, Maddy,' she says. 'After church. In the daytime. I'll talk to you then.'

18

The books are glowing.

Lit by a circle of pale yellow light from my bedside table, the leather covers look bronze and shimmery, not cracked and brown. I can't take my eyes off them – what if they spring open and scatter their pages on the floor, or fly through the air and attack me like a flock of evil birds?

One of them is open on the bed in front of me – the slimmest volume, the only one written in a language that looks anything like English. I should have waited until morning, until Hannah came back from church and it was *safe,* but I couldn't resist, and now I wish I had.

The pages are made of thick yellow parchment and the exact, square-ish lettering has been written by hand. But it's the picture that grabs my throat and squeezes the air out of my lungs.

A raging fire, lighting up a dark, inky sky. Figures – women with thick flowing hair and long shift dresses showing bare shoulders that look as if they've been slashed or gored or –

A horrible thought occurs to me – is this the image that appeared on my laptop? The one I thought I'd imagined?

I swallow hard, forcing myself to look.

No. These lines are thicker, more distinct. I lean in closely; touch the paper with trembling fingers, as if that could keep what I'm seeing from jumping off the page and escaping into my room.

Creatures – horrible-looking devils with bat-like wings and snaky, pointed tongues – stand amongst the women, their faces turned into ugly, jeering smiles. Above them, the night sky is awash with light – vapoury strands. And below them are the words . . .

Be it that outwardlie visions are nowe ceased, all spirites that appeares are euill.

Visions. Appear. I get that much.

Euill . . .

Something churns in my stomach.

Evil?

I turn the page.

They converse naturallie with them whom they hauntes.

Spirits, haunt – is the book talking about ghosts?

Guiltie of greeuous offences

wicked and damned spirites

Was it not euill for the angell of the deuill to decieue simple ignorantes.

My heart pounds. I think about what Hannah asked me – am I afraid of words on pages?

Yes. I'm afraid of *these* pages, *these* words. The *deuill* – that's the devil. G*uilty. Wicked. Damned.* Is that me? I'm the one who sees ghosts, so am I the *simple ignorante* who is deceived?

I turn to another page, even though I'm terrified of what it might tell me.

Amongst the sortes of spirites that followes certaine persons, there is one more monstrous than the reste.

Suddenly, I'm aware of how quiet it is. Without the storms and thunder I can hear every crack in the shifting walls, each dog barking in the distance, every twitch of the curtains in my draughty room.

There is one more monstrous than the reste . . .

A creak on my staircase – I hear that, too.

Footsteps.

I hear breathing, shuffling sounds, a quiet knock on the door.

I hold my breath, put my hands across my chest to muffle the sound of my heartbeats.

Tap, tap, tap.

I sit up with a start, gasping. Why did I go into that room with Hannah? Why did I open this book?

'Maddy?' A ghostly whisper.

I say nothing. If I don't answer, if I don't breathe, it might –

'Maddy, are you there?'

I cover my face with my hand, stifling a sob, willing whatever it is to go away so that I can breathe again, so that I won't die of fright.

'Maddy, it's me, Darshan.'

I let out a huge sigh. I slip out of bed, unlock the door, open it slowly, checking carefully to make sure that it's really him, that it's not some devil creature pretending to be a timid little –

Of course, it's Darshan. And standing beside him, silently weeping, is Jordan.

I open the door and both boys stumble into my room.

Jordan's teeth are chattering, but he's dressed warmly enough – slippers, pyjamas, plaid woollen dressing gown – so he can't be that cold.

'Jordan had an accident,' Darshan whispers.

'What?' I ask. 'Are you hurt?'

'No,' Darshan whispers. 'An accident. Like, a *toilet* accident.'

'I wet myself,' Jordan blubs.

'Oh, Jordan,' I say, 'everybody wets the bed sometime.' I try to put my arm around him, but he pulls away.

'I didn't wet the bed,' he protests. 'I woke up. I was wide awake. I needed the toilet – I was desperate for it, but . . .'

'He wouldn't go to the loo,' Darshan says.

Jordan looks down at the floor, as if he's ashamed.

'He says there was a man in the toilet.'

'A man? Like Mr Casey?'

Jordan shakes his head.

'He says it was a scary man.'

Jordan sniffs and Darshan clears his throat.

'He says it was *very* scary. Every scarier than the *fings*.'

19

I zip up my sweatshirt and chew a piece of cold dry toast.

The refectory is nearly empty. Jordan and Darshan are clearing away their breakfast trays, and shoving them through the serving hatch. Jordan's eyes look sunken and his face seems a bit pale, but he and Darsh are laughing and joking. The terrors of last night seem to have faded now that it's morning and the sun is streaming through the high windows.

I helped them look for the scary man before they went back to bed, but there was no one in the toilets, nobody in the broom cupboard or lurking in the corridors, nothing hiding under Jordan's or Darshan's beds.

Not last night anyway, at least not where we were looking.

And while I was pretending to be brave and showing the boys there was nothing to be scared of, the words from the book never left my head: *There is one more monstrous than the reste . . .*

I check the door – Hannah's church bus from Crowham village will be back soon. Once I've talked to her about what

117

I read in that book, I'll feel better. Maybe she'll have the answers to my questions. Maybe she knows what everything means.

At the table nearest the window a group of Year 10 girls cluster around Caleb. He's sitting next to Nat Ashmore, of course – smiling at her, touching her leg underneath the table. Why does he have to do that? Where everyone can see?

Yuck.

I drain the last drop of tea from my mug and wipe my hands on the legs of my jeans. I reach under my T-shirt and take out a book that's hidden there. It's another volume from the secret library, the title so faded I can't read the words, or symbols, or whatever they are.

I open the book to a thick, yellowed, rough-edged page. I look at the door again. *Come on, Hannah. Hurry!*

More pictures – rough etchings, like the ones that Mr Casey showed us in his history slide show. I can only make out a few of the words – *reuenge, murther, deuillishe practises* – but the pictures tell a clear enough story, and there are captions – dates, places, names – underneath the gory images.

One picture is of scaly-bodied devils who dance around a fire with people wearing flowing, hooded cloaks. The caption says, *Verrie merrie Crowham necromancy.*

Crowham? As in – Crowham, Sussex? As in *here?*

I turn the page, my fingers trembling. Here's another etching of a blazing fire, but instead of dancing women there's a tiny robed figure being led toward the flames.

Sacrifice of the deuills childe, it says.

I lean forward to get a closer look at the picture. The fire is in a circular clearing, surrounded by tall, dense trees.

My stomach flips. It looks just like Crowham Wood.

In the picture a hideous creature stands near the edge of the trees, watching what's also taking place – a woman tied to a stake, flames leaping around her body. The creature's laughing. His horrid grimace shows pointed, fang-like teeth, and his eyes are huge and wolfish.

I close my eyes and listen for the sound of screaming, the smell of fire. This must be related to what I've been hearing – the horrible grinding, the crackling flames. But now there's nothing, just Nat Ashmore's irritating giggle, the clang of pans and pots being put away in the kitchen.

I look again at the picture of the burning woman. The print underneath it is blurred, making the caption impossible to read without having to squint or put my face up to the page.

Cwhm. —1515. Alice D— W—

That's all I can make out. The rest of the numbers and letters have been scratched from the surface of the paper, scraped off with a needle or the tip of a knife.

'Looks fascinating, Maddy.'

I sit up straight, my heart pounding, and slowly close the book. Caleb's standing across the table from me.

'It's n-not, actually,' I stammer. 'It's total rubbish.'

He saunters around to my side of the table.

'Seriously,' he says. 'I love old books. Where did you find it?'

I push my chair back and stand up, the book tucked securely under one arm. Why is he asking these questions? Does he know about the library, too?

'Sorry,' I mutter. 'Gotta go.'

I try to pass Caleb, eyes on the floor, but he steps in front of me. Even without looking at him, I sense that electric charge, that weird, Taser-like pulse I felt on the stage the day I collapsed.

'Wait a minute. We need to talk.'

As I back away, I catch my heel on one of the chair legs. Caleb reaches out to catch me before I fall.

'Hey.' My arm throbs where he clutches it. I try not to flinch, try not to let him know what I just felt. Once I've got my balance again, I shield my body with the book, clutching it in front of me with both hands.

'Go back to your girlfriend,' I say, looking straight at him for once.

He stares back without blinking, still holding my arm, and for the first time I notice that his irises are flecked with bits of green and gold, like mine are, except that his eyes are brilliant blue and mine are muddy grey.

He's not gazing into *my* eyes, though, he's checking out the rest of my face – my nose, my chin, the line of my jaw. Is this a game he's playing with Natalie and the others? I glance over at their table – sure enough, they're all watching and sniggering. Maybe Caleb's going to give me a rating – marks out of ten.

On the other side of the room a door swings open, bashing hard against the wall. Some of the kids from Hannah's church bus barrel into the refectory. I pull away from Caleb, clutching the book even tighter, and head for the door while more kids hurry past me and rush up to the serving counter.

'This isn't a restaurant,' Mrs Gibson growls at them. She bangs a ladle against a metal pot. 'I'm not here at your beck and call.'

While I wait at the door a little girl – the one who arrived the same day as Darshan and Jordan – tugs at my arm. 'Hannah's not here.'

'I can see that,' I say distractedly, looking out into the corridor.

'Hannah's gone home.'

'What?'

The girl ambles over to the serving queue. I look at the table of older boys. Conor Kelly's in our year – he'll be the one to ask.

'Conor?' I have to shout over the sound of dirty plates being stacked on the conveyor belts, and breakfasts being wolfed down. 'Do you know where Hannah is?'

Conor wipes his face with a serviette. 'Africa,' he shouts back.

'Ha ha, Conor. Very funny.'

'No, seriously, she went back to Africa.'

My eyes widen. My stomach twists with dread. 'What?'

'That's what the driver told us.'

'That's not possible,' I say.

'But that's what the headmaster told *him*,' Conor says.

'Well then, the headmaster is a liar.'

My voice gets louder as the refectory suddenly goes quiet. Mrs Gibson has stopped bashing and barking. The other kids stop talking. I can feel the room get bigger – the stained-glass windows expand, the ceiling raises itself, the floorboards shift and shake, stretching out underneath me.

'She wouldn't have just left,' I say, my voice trembling.

Everybody's watching me. I cling to the book, desperate to stay on my feet, desperate to keep from crying. 'She wouldn't have gone without saying goodbye.'

I'm sitting on a narrow pew outside the headmaster's office. Apparently Mr Grayling heard about my outburst in the refectory this morning and didn't appreciate being called a liar by one of his students. *That sort of talk is bad for the younger ones,* it said in the message that was delivered by a prefect. *It's unsettling.*

A ghost slips out from under the carpet, the shimmery one from the night in the medical room, the kindly one.

I shake my head. *She,* I think. *Kindly –* how stupid is that? What was it Hannah said – that the ghosts are here to protect me? *From what?* I think, and then I remember the books she took – *we* took – from that secret library.

The pictures flash into my eyes – the dancing in the clearing, the burning woman, the child. Is that the *badness?* Is that what Hannah can see? Is that why she's gone?

I tried her mobile this morning – I managed to get a bar of signal – but it didn't even ring. Did that mean she'd already got on the plane? Was she out of the country? Could it happen that fast?

Then I checked her room. It was unlocked, whatever that meant. All her drawers were empty and the safari posters had been taken from the walls, but everything was still a mess, with cupboard doors left open and the bed unmade.

And where were the books? I looked everywhere I could think of – in her wardrobe, under her bed, even behind the pipes in the bathroom sink – but they'd disappeared, too.

The door to the headmaster's office creaks open and Mr Grayling calls me inside. He closes the door behind me and I see that we're not alone.

Missy's here. Mr Casey, too. What's this got to do with them?

The headmaster clears his throat. 'I don't like being dragged away from my Sunday lunch, but we felt it best to explain your friend's departure, in light of the upset you caused in the refectory this morning.'

Missy stands as straight and still as a prison guard, and I'm aware of other noises in the background – a ticking clock, the fluorescent light humming overhead, a whoosh of ghosts beneath my chair. It's time to beg forgiveness, I suppose. Time to throw myself on the mercy of the court.

'I shouldn't have called you a liar,' I mutter. 'At least not until you had the chance to tell me the truth about Hannah.'

'The truth?' Mr Grayling says. 'Is that what you want?'

My heart's fluttering. I don't know what I'm expecting him to say – that Hannah's been snatched by a sinister cult, maybe. That a coven of Crowham Wood witches wants to become more ethnically diverse.

I'm expecting something about monsters or demons. *Badness.*

Mr Grayling sighs indulgently. 'Hannah was homesick.'

'She wanted to see her family,' Missy says. 'It happens a lot – you know that. Remember your friend Severine last year?'

My eyes sting with tears. Of course I do.

'How she went back to France in the middle of the term? And Olga from Russia? One day she was here, the next . . .'

Missy holds up her arms and waves her hands like she's trying to demonstrate how easily friends – mine, anyway – can vanish into thin air.

'So where did she go?' I ask.

'Back to her parents in Cape Town,' Mr Casey says. 'Hannah was too upset to say goodbye to you, so her aunt collected her after church this morning and they went straight to the airport.'

'Her aunt?'

'Her aunt Patience,' Missy says. 'Her mother's sister. She lives in London.'

'I see,' I say, but of course I don't. Hannah told me her parents were working in Rwanda, not South Africa. And she never said a word about having an aunt living in England, or about feeling homesick. Are they just making this up? But why would they lie?

'So do you have this aunt's phone number?' I ask. 'An e-mail address?' I'm about to tell them that Hannah's mobile wasn't working, but something stops me – the stomach-twisting feeling that I shouldn't say another word about Hannah, that something here is very wrong.

Missy steps forward. 'Of course, we have her number. I'll have someone from records jot it down for you first thing tomorrow morning.'

The headmaster tuts and sighs. The clock strikes twice for half past, a muffled gong. A ghost swooshes through a crack in the floorboards.

Mr Casey holds the door open for me and almost pushes me out of the room. No one tells me they're sorry about Hannah, nobody asks me how it makes me feel that she just up and left.

I creep back out into the gloomy vestibule and look up at the pictures of the old, dead men. Their black beady eyes seem to watch me, their faces mock and sneer like those terrible devils in the books Hannah showed me – snarling, laughing.

A ghost shimmies up the wall, and slips behind a picture frame.

I can see ghosts.

My heart sinks when I remember those words, the dread in my stomach twists tighter. Why did I say them? Why didn't I listen to Mum's warning and keep my stupid mouth shut?

I told Hannah about the ghosts, and now she's gone. Whatever's happened to her, wherever she is – it's all my fault.

I eat dinner in my room – lukewarm mac and cheese that tastes like salted cardboard. I couldn't bear going down to the refectory on my own.

Without Hannah.

But the sounds of a normal Sunday night are upsetting, too. They waft up from the corridor below my stairs – tinny music, wonky scales practiced on a squeaking clarinet, the hysterical laughter of girls whose mates haven't disappeared or suddenly gone home without saying goodbye.

After the meeting in Mr Grayling's office I trudged to the end of the driveway and tried to pick up a mobile signal. Nothing. I went through the gates and walked as far as the main road – the buses don't go on a Sunday, so my only other option was to cut through the forest if I wanted to get to town and make it back before dark.

I never found a signal. I tried Hannah's number again, but there was nothing – no hissing or static or long beeping tones.

Just silence. And now I wish I'd had the courage to go into the woods.

I creep down my narrow staircase, and carry the tray of food remains past the other girls' bedrooms. When I get to the end of the corridor, Natalie Ashmore comes out of the bathroom, fresh from the shower, wearing a snow white towelling robe. I stop in my tracks to avoid bumping into her, but the plate of stodgy macaroni slides off my tray, and the half-full mug of tea clatters on to the floor and smashes, splattering Nat with liquid sludge.

She lets out an ear-piercing scream.

'Can't you be more careful?'

I set the tray on the floor and try to gather up the macaroni chunks and bits of broken mug. I'm ready to grovel, I'm about to say 'Sorry,' but something stops me and I stand up without saying a word, leaving the tray and the bits of food where they fell. I feel the strangest power, if that's the word. It's like the weird energy between Caleb and me, only this time it's inside my body, coursing through my veins.

'Did you say something?' I ask. I step forward, feeling slightly off-balance.

Natalie backs away, wrapping her dressing gown around her body. She looks at me warily and when she speaks there's none of her usual sarcastic tone.

'I'm sorry about your friend.'

She steps back again. 'That Hannah's gone home. You know. Left like that . . . so suddenly. Must be tough.'

My eyes prickle with tears, but the shock of Natalie Ashmore being kind – actually sounding like she cares – helps me keep my composure.

On my way back from the refectory, I take the shortcut through the dimly lit admin corridor. Those gruesome pictures of old dead men still glower at me, but this time I glower right back. A narrow strip of light bleeds from underneath one of the office doors. Somebody must be working late, or left a light on by mistake.

I read the sign on the door – *School Records.*

That's where they keep medical information and phone numbers and contact details for the students. There's bound to be a file on Hannah – maybe I can find out where she's gone, maybe I can get an address for this aunt without having to wait for Missy. And if what they said is true – if she was too upset to say goodbye – then she'll definitely want to hear from me, right?

I try the door.

The handle turns; it's been left unlocked.

'Hello?' I whisper. I open the door. 'Anybody here?'

No answer. I step into the room and close the door behind me, turning the key to lock myself in. There's a battered metal cabinet in one of the corners, with files sorted in alphabetical order: A-E, F-J, K-O –

M for Masupha.

The drawer squeaks and groans, but it opens. I rummage until I find a brand-new folder with Hannah's name on it. I take it to the desk, hold it under the light.

Hannah's picture – a grainy black and white passport photo with her date of birth scrawled on the back – is stapled to a single sheet of paper. There's the address of her old school in Cape Town – St Rose Convent Academy – but it's been crossed out. There's an address in Rwanda – 325 27KN Road, Kigali – and underneath is a phone number with a long overseas code, next to her parents' names, Theboho and John Masupha-Harris.

The rest is blank. All the other sections are empty. There's no family name in Cape Town, no UK contact – there's definitely no name or number for an aunt living in England.

So does this prove that Missy was lying?

The half-digested macaroni in my stomach churns and my teeth chatter, as I put the papers back into the cabinet and close the drawer. I creep back out to the corridor, my heart pounding.

It's only when I get to the entrance hall that I see anyone else. It's Missy – standing in front of the huge fireplace, wearing her hooded dressing gown, facing the flames. I wait in the open doorway for her to turn around and challenge me, accuse me of some terrible crime, drag me to the fire as a punishment, like one of the hooded figures in the devil book.

The air stirs when I close the door and the delicate glass in the chandelier tinkles. But Missy doesn't hear it. She stays completely still, hypnotised, entranced by the bright flames that dance and whirl and crackle with life.

'Missy?'

When she turns to me she puts her hands to her face and gasps, staring wide-eyed in shock.

'Miss Burke?' I say, louder this time.

She shakes her head and blinks as she comes back to reality. 'Oh, it's *you*, Madeline.'

'Of course it's me,' I say. 'And I'm called Maddy . . .'

She adjusts her dressing gown and steps away from the fire. 'Glad we got everything sorted about Hannah. Back to her family. How lovely for her.'

She still looks half-dazed, like a sleepwalker who hasn't quite woken up. I nod, and shuffle past her to the stairs. When I reach the mezzanine level I look down. She's facing the fire again, swaying back and forth, like she's dancing to music that only she can hear.

22

The sparkly ghost is at the foot of my bed, stretched out like a glittery, translucent cat. I'm tempted to lean over and stroke it, see if it will purr.

It's way past midnight. I'm looking through the devil books again, randomly flicking through pages, hoping I'll find a clue about Hannah – that some image will jump out at me and things will make sense.

The pictures jump out all right – hideous demons, dancing witches, people dressed like Missy in long, hooded cloaks – but nothing makes sense. How could it? My best friend's disappeared and people are lying.

I turn the pages to a picture of trees. A dark, dense forest, with tall, pointy pines. I remember how Hannah was so afraid in Crowham Wood. Not in the library, not in the dark corridors – just in the forest. What was it she saw there? What kind of *badness?* What was she going to tell me when she got back from church?

I turn to another page, but the pictures are getting blurry, the books unbearably heavy. I climb out of bed and dump them in the bottom of my wardrobe. I hide them under the pile of dirty laundry and weigh everything down with a layer of shoes and boots and old school bags.

I tuck myself back into bed. Funny how everything's different, although everything looks the same – the Californian posters, the sloping ceilings, the half-open drawers stuffed full of socks and tights.

When Hannah asked me why I was put up here in the attic I didn't tell her how I really felt about it, because I thought she might laugh.

Safe.

Secure. Untouchable. And I knew if there were any problems with the other students or the teachers, I could always talk to Missy. She was like a surrogate mum to me, or a kindly aunt at least.

And then I had Hannah. A proper friend. One who wasn't going to leave me behind after a few months, like Severine or Olga did, just when we were getting to know each other, just when we having fun, sneaking out of our rooms at night and wandering the corridors.

I close my eyes but those pictures from the books – witches and demons – spin in my head like images from an old-fashioned zoetrope machine, moving faster and faster until they spring to life. And in the middle of the pictures – trying to break free from the pages – is Hannah, her body trembling, her mouth open in a silent scream.

I shake myself awake, but other thoughts overwhelm me – where is Hannah? In some horrible place?

I try to remember what everyone's told me – *I know who you are. Don't be scared.* Maybe these things are connected, like Hannah said.

Badness. Fings. Horrifying noises, upsetting dreams . . .

That weird energy between Caleb and me. Missy swaying in front of the fire. Hannah disappearing.

I squeeze my eyes shut, trying to blank out those pictures from the devil book, trying to forget the words.

There is one more monstrous than the reste.

I cut through the churchyard, the tall grass heavy with early morning dew, and creep up the overgrown path to the entrance. The gravestones surrounding me tilt forwards, as if they're too tired to stand upright. Fat ghosts, like gossamer sponges, hover in the shadows.

The church is locked so I follow the path to the side door,

glancing behind me as I round the corner. Who am I expecting to see? Missy? Caleb? Someone who followed me as I slipped out the back door before breakfast, and clambered over the fence behind the far playing fields?

I take out my phone. There's a decent signal here, so I try Hannah's mobile number. Nothing. Totally dead.

I look into a narrow leaded window and jiggle the heavy iron door handle. It's dark inside, but I push the door until it creaks open. When I take my hand away, my fingers are filthy with dirt and grit. I brush them on the back of my jeans and see what I've accidentally uncovered.

There's a marking on the window frame. A huge claw mark inside a circle – like the ones Hannah showed me in Crowham village that day. I pull the door shut, my heart pounding. I can't go in there. What if some creature is waiting for me – something I've seen or read about in the books – something *monstrous*?

No, I think, leaning against the door until my breathing slows down. These marks mean nothing – they're just weird architectural features like gargoyles or fancy roof tiles. We saw dozens of these in the village, and the shops were totally normal, no matter what Hannah thought – of course the church would have them too.

I open the door again, and creep down the dark, musty-smelling corridor, guided by a dim pool of light that's seeping underneath a heavy curtain.

'Hello?' I call. 'Is anybody here?'

When I push the curtains aside it's like looking into a dark cave. So much for churches being comforting, I think. So much for thinking they'd be warm and safe.

Gradually, my eyes adjust, and I see a tiny side chapel tucked away to my right. There's a dark bronze figure behind a metal stand full of tiny candles and flickering flames.

I reach into my pocket and take out some change – isn't that what you're meant to do in these places? Say a prayer? I put twenty pence in the slot, light a candle and look up at the statue. At first it looks like some random saint holding a walking stick. Then I see he's got massive angel wings, folded at his back, and the stick is actually a spear. I move closer, bend over to read the tarnished bronze plate.

Under the statue's feet, something moves.

I step back, gasping. There it is again – a glimmer of movement, a ripple of colour. My heart's pounding, and I remember the strange dark light I saw in the church window the first time Hannah and I came into the village. Is this what I'm seeing? Is this one of Jordan's *fings?*

Something shakes and slithers. Tiny red eyes glow, searching me out.

A serpent. Huge-fanged, coiled and ready to spring.

I take another step back – this can't be real – and catch my foot on the candle stand. I tumble to the floor, and curl up into a ball, waiting for snake to attack or the fire from the candles to set me alight.

At the far end of the church, a door creaks open.

Shuffling footsteps echo through the church, and finally a voice rings out.

'St Michael.' The words bounce off the rough-plastered walls and flagstone floors. 'St Michael, Archangel and Protector.'

I crawl back on to my feet and look at the statue. Nothing's moving, of course. Tangles of angry, bronze snakes with tiny jewelled eyes are trapped underneath the angel's feet. What an idiot I am. I can almost imagine Hannah watching from some hiding place, hear her laughing at me for being scared of a statue in a church.

'St Michael's our patron saint, but I'm sure you already knew that.'

The footsteps coming up the central aisle belong to Reverend Anne, the vicar. She's wearing trainers and jeans and an ordinary grey cardigan over her black priest's top.

'You go to the school, don't you?'

I take the hand that she's holding out. How does she know I go to Crowham?

'Don't worry,' she says. 'I won't report you for truancy, Maddy.'

How does she know my *name?*

'Maddy Deeprose,' she says, smiling. 'Year 8. I know all about you.'

My heart flutters – that's exactly what Mr Casey said.

'I'm not stalking you,' she laughs. 'You don't need to look so nervous. I know about *everyone* at the school – that's part of my job.'

'Well, you know about my friend, then,' I say. 'She's gone missing.'

'Sounds serious,' Reverend Anne says. 'What's your friend's name?'

'Hannah.' I feel my throat tighten and tears spring into my eyes. 'Hannah Masupha-Harris . . .'

Suddenly, it's all too much – the worry, the fear – and I can't say any more, I can only flutter my hands in front of my face, as if that will shoo away the tears that are streaming down my cheeks.

'Sorry,' I sputter. 'It's just . . .'

Reverend Anne puts an arm around my shoulder and leads me to the front pews. 'There, there, Maddy,' she says. Her voice reminds me of Mum's – the gentle way she shushed me when I was little – and that makes me sob even harder.

Eventually the musky smells, the dim light and Reverend

Anne's kindness manage to calm me down. When I stand up again, the sun is shining through the stained-glass window behind the statue. It's another image of St Michael – only this time his huge white wings are unfurled and he's swooping to the ground like a mighty eagle, brandishing a sword that sends out beams of red, yellow and purple light.

'See?' Reverend Anne says. 'It's better already.'

'They told me Hannah went home to South Africa with her aunt, without bothering to say goodbye.'

The vicarage kitchen looks like a miniature version of the Crowham refectory, with a high-beamed ceiling and a battered trestle table, but the tea is better and the cakes made by Reverend Anne are as light and airy as Mrs Gibson's are thick and leaden.

'Well, that's good, isn't it? You must be terribly upset that she left so suddenly, but doesn't that prove she's safe?'

Reverend Anne adds more water to the blue and white striped teapot.

'Except Hannah doesn't have an aunt – not that she ever told me about, anyway, and her parents aren't in Cape Town, they're somewhere in Rwanda . . .'

The tears come again, so Reverend Anne reaches across the table for the box of tissues, and hands one to me.

'Everybody's lying,' I sniff. 'That's why I came here.'

Reverend Anne gives the tea a stir with a big wooden spoon.

'Well, I don't know any more than you do, Maddy, because I didn't see what happened after church, but I'm willing to listen if there's anything else you want to tell me – about Hannah. About you.'

I'm not sure if it's because she's being so kind or if it's because she's a vicar, or because her voice sounds so much like Mum's, but I feel safe with Reverend Anne in this lovely, warm kitchen. I want to tell her everything about the school, not just Hannah – about Caleb and devil books and Missy acting weird.

'If I tell you the truth, you'll think we're crazy – Hannah and me.'

'I won't.'

Reverend Anne stays still, waiting patiently for me to speak, her face set in a soft, calm expression.

'Well, Hannah could see stuff. Kind of see it, anyway – invisible stuff.'

Reverend Anne nods patiently, while I gather the courage to keep talking. I notice how quiet it is – a clock ticks in another room and birds are squawking in the huge trees outside.

'*Badness*,' I say. 'That's what Hannah called it – *badness*. She didn't seem scared or anything – she's very brave – but it is definitely something real to her. And she said it was in the village and in the school and all around Crowham. And she said she would tell me about it when she got back from church . . .'

I stop talking, wipe my eyes, blow my nose.

I expect Reverend Anne to get annoyed with me for being silly or telling tales, but her kind expression doesn't change. 'And what about you, Maddy? Can you see . . . stuff?'

I take a deep breath, but before I can utter a word, a car pulls into the driveway and toots its horn.

'Ach, that's my family – talk about bad timing.'

A man opens the door and two little boys bounce into the kitchen. One's carrying a school bag from nursery, the other one is toddling behind him.

'Mummy! Mummy!' The boys clamber on to Reverend Anne's lap, giggling, fighting for the best perch. They look like their dad, who lumbers in behind them – gingery hair, freckles, blue eyes.

'Hang on, boys,' Reverend Anne says. 'We have a guest.'

Her husband drops his bags of shopping on the table.

'Tom Preston,' he says, holding out his hand for me to shake.

'I'm Maddy,' I say.

'Maddy?' The man – Tom – looks at Reverend Anne with his eyebrows raised.

'Maddy *Deeprose*,' Reverend Anne says. 'A friend of Hannah's.'

She says each word slowly. 'You know, *Hannah* from the *school*.'

'Ah, yes,' Tom sighs, 'Maddy. Hannah.'

He's talking oddly, too – it's like he knows who I am, like they've had this conversation before.

'Hannah's gone missing, according to Maddy,' Reverend Anne says calmly. 'The school says that Hannah's aunt collected her after church, but Maddy's not convinced –'

'Because she doesn't have an aunt . . .' I interrupt.

'So Maddy's come here . . .'

The youngest boy squirms off Reverend Anne's lap. She ruffles his head, and motions for all the boys to go into another room. They must be used this, I think. Being sidelined all the time, having their mother's attention taken up with more urgent matters, like life and death and God and –

'What else did Hannah say about this *badness*, Maddy?'

Tom coughs and sputters. His forehead looks scrunched with worry, and he pulls his chair closer to the table.

'We were walking through Crowham Wood one night.'

'Whoa . . . that was brave,' Tom blurts out.

'Shhh . . . come on, Tom, this must be frightening enough for Maddy, without you –'

'Well, would *you* go there after dark? That collar around your neck can't protect you from everything, darling.'

It's hard to tell if Tom's being serious or making a joke. He doesn't smile or wink, and he seems too kind and gentle to wind me up just for fun.

'And we saw a dog.'

Reverend Anne nods. 'That's not unusual, is it?'

'But Hannah was so scared of it, even though she tried not to show it. And the dog seemed scared, too. It stood still and looked into the woods and stopped barking. And I was worried about it – thought it might be sick – but Hannah didn't care because . . .'

I sigh, trying to remember what she called it.

'She gave it name, like Toto, in *The Wizard of Oz* . . . Toko-something?'

'Good Lord,' Tom mutters. 'Thought we'd heard the last of that character.'

Reverend Anne smiles at me. 'Tom and I were missionaries in Lesotho –'

'That's where Hannah's mum is from, and she's a missionary, too.'

'Yes,' Tom says. 'We lived in the same part of the country as Hannah's mum and dad. We knew them –'

Reverend Anne clears her throat and Tom stops talking. 'Just to say hello to,' she says. 'Isn't that right, darling?'

Reverend Anne looks over at her husband, who's nodding in agreement.

'So who's this Toko, anyway?' I ask.

'Tokoloshe is a sort of southern African bogey man,' Reverend Anne says. 'He gets blamed for all sorts of things – disappearing animals, a poor corn crop. For an African child, Toko would be a terrifying creature.'

'Well, Hannah was sure scared of it,' I say. 'When we got back to school she told me to keep my legs off the floor, in case Toko grabbed them or something.'

'Did Hannah tell you anything more?'

I think about the secret library. About *showing* me the *badness* – what would happen if I told Reverend Anne and her husband? I know I'm not allowed to talk about ghosts, but the library and the books – they're different, aren't they? They'd believe me about the *badness* if I told them about those devil pictures. And talking to a vicar – a priest – isn't that more like confessing than telling?

In one of the other rooms, somebody starts to cry. It must be one of the little boys, but Reverend Anne takes no notice. She's probably used to this kind of interruption.

'Right,' she says, 'time for another cuppa, and then we need to think about getting you back to school.' The tea she pours from the pot has grown brown and stewy, with a film on top.

Tom clears his throat. 'I'm sure you can help Maddy get to the bottom of this, can't you, dear?'

The crying from the other room's getting louder, but Reverend Anne and her husband still don't react.

'After all, why would anybody lie?' Tom asks.

'Because they've done something to her,' I say.

I have to shout to be heard – the crying is getting so loud, so close. I wonder why they're still oblivious until I realise that it's not a child and the sound isn't coming from inside the house.

'Done something?'

It's a woman – and she's in my head, wailing in terror, shrieking with pain – and before I can say anything else a wall of voices hits me like a powerful wave, and I'm overcome by the sounds of screaming and shouting and pitiful sobs.

I slump forward on to the table, covering my head with my arms.

'Maddy? Are you all right?'

The voices hush for a moment, so I push myself upright, desperate to get back to where I was. But then a face floats in front of me – no proper features, just a sad, pale shape and when the voices come back I push my hands over my ears, and slump down again.

'Tom!' Reverend Anne is shouting. 'Help me.'

Her strong arms hold me, supporting my body before it slides away.

A man's voice hisses back. 'I told you there'd be trouble if we got involved with this, Annie. We've got two kids – you should've listened.'

As the world gets darker I hear Reverend Anne. 'How could I say no to them, Tom? How could I –'

Those are the last of her words I hear.

Something pulls me away from the warm kitchen and drags me into another place – a cold, silent night of trees and mud.

I stumble blindly. No more screaming, no more sobs.

I breathe. White, heaving puffs billow into the frozen air like ghosts.

And I hear my name –

Madeline.

A voice is calling to me – the wailing woman's voice.

Child, child . . .

Bright lights cut through the darkness – blue, yellow, red – and there's shouting again, and the crying voice sounds like Reverend Anne.

I feel a sharp shock of pain – the prick of a needle.

And then I'm gone.

24

I open my eyes to dull grey light, and gauzy half-awake vision.

Disoriented, I struggle out of bed – it's a huge drop to the floor. I cross cold tiles on bare feet and look out the window.

Where am I?

A dark grey sea shimmers far, far below me. Is this Venice Beach? Catalina?

A massive jetty – lit by carnival lights of red, yellow and blue – juts out into the water. There's a narrow strip of stony beach, a long paved boardwalk, old-fashioned iron lamp posts, with lights strung between them like illuminated pearls.

I crane my neck, trying to see a bit more, and there's my answer, written in huge lit-up letters.

Brighton Pier

I turn back to my bed, noticing for the first time the walled sides, the crisp white sheets, the foldaway tray at the foot of the bed.

I must be in hospital. The Royal Sussex.

Just as I start to remember what happened – another funny turn, with noises and voices saying words I can't remember – I hear footsteps in the corridor and a man-shaped figure stands in the doorway, blocking the light.

'You shouldn't be on your feet,' he says, stepping into the room.

He goes to the edge of my bed, clicks something on the netbook he's holding. I breathe a sigh of relief – he must be a doctor.

'Maddy Deeprose,' he says, smiling. Even in the dark room I can see white teeth, bright eyes. He's impossibly handsome – Caleb handsome, but older, with lighter hair.

'I'm not ill,' I say, shuffling back towards the bed.

He looks at the netbook. 'You've been asleep for almost twelve hours.'

I inch myself on to the bed, pull the gown over my knees before lifting up my legs.

'Since your teacher brought you in this morning.'

'My teacher?'

He clicks the screen. 'A Miss Burke, I believe.'

'Oh, her,' I say, vaguely. I smile and nod, even though I know that can't be true. I was at the church, not school. I don't remember much, but I know I was looking for Hannah, and Reverend Anne was the one who shouted for an ambulance.

Why is this doctor saying it was Missy?

'We've done some scans and they've all been clear. We want to keep an eye on you for a few more days, though. See if we can find out why you keep passing out. I've informed the school.'

He smiles. Moves closer to the bed.

'Do they want to lock me away or something?' I say. 'Is that was this is all about – are they saying I'm mad?'

He touches my hand reassuringly.

'We'll run more tests, Maddy. That's all.'

As he pats my wrist a memory tugs at my brain. It nearly comes to me, but what is it? The clifftop in my dreams, being dragged through a dark forest –

I look down at the doctor's hand. Beneath the skin, I see a shimmery, snaky glow.

He chuckles as I pull my arm away.

'Don't worry, Maddy,' he laughs. 'Everything will be fine.'

As soon as he's gone, I clamber out of bed and open the locker in the corner of the room. I expect it to be empty, but my clothes are on hangers and nothing's been taken from my bag – here's my mobile, here's my purse.

The bars show a strong signal. I try Hannah's number again, but it's still off.

I run through the home screen. Maybe she texted or left a message.

No texts. Three voicemails waiting.

I listen to the first one.

'Please do not hang up. Your number has been randomly selected . . .'

The next message is from Mum.

'Honey? Honey, it's Mummy. I'm so sorry, darling, I'm so –'

Her voice is slurred. Has she been drinking? She's babbling on about being a rubbish mum and a how a real mother would be with her daughter all the time and wouldn't have sent her off to some –

And then she sobs.

Still, I let the message play out. It's comforting to hear her voice, even if it's just a recording, and even if she's not making much sense.

'Oh, sorry, sweetheart,' she sniffs. 'I shouldn't have said that, what a daft thing to . . . of course I'm a real mother, it's just that you're so far away and I feel so –'

She breaks down again, but manages to choke out a few more words.

'I'll fly over – the minute we're done filming, yeah? London?

A week together – just you and me, darling – I'll rent a flat. How does that sound?'

'That sounds good, Mum,' I say to the message.

'Or you could bring your new friend along – what's her name – Hannah?'

'Yes, Mum,' I say. 'Hannah.'

I stop the message. What's the point of listening? She's not really there.

One more. The call was made three hours ago. Private number, it says, whatever that means.

There's only static. A mistake, obviously. Some numpty hasn't locked their phone so it's calling random numbers without them knowing.

Then I hear breathing – a mouth close to the phone, like a perv or a crank call. Somebody speaks, but what are they saying? There are too many sounds in the background, weird thuds, pounding, punching –

A familiar voice, even if it's hollow and distorted. 'Maddy, it's me.'

I take a deep breath, hardly daring to believe what I'm hearing. I slump down, hiding behind the cupboard door, cradling the phone against my face with both hands, as if it needs protecting.

'It's Hannah.'

That's what the words sound like, anyway, but there's too much static, it's so crackly. I keep listening, struggling to make out the words that rise out of the scratchy hum.

'Dark.'

Everything's muddled up, but I think that's what she said.

'Trees.'

More thudding, a rumble, like thunder, a shrill cat-like shriek. Too many noises, it doesn't make sense.

'Don't trust them.'

A scream.

Hannah's?

And another.

My heart sinks. *Yes, Hannah's.*

Then the crunching of footsteps and a crackling, like fire.

I creep down the emergency stairs, treading like a cat, not making a sound.

I take out my phone, listen to Hannah's message again, but I can't make out anything new. It's definitely Hannah who's screaming, though, definitely her voice saying the few words I can make out, her words telling me not to trust them.

I make it to the first landing, then another flight of stairs, then another landing that's lit with a sickly yellow safety light, then another and another until, finally, I'm opening a heavy fire door that says, *Ground Floor. A & E.*

The place is teeming with people. Nurses rush past with piled-up folders of notes, porters heave massive trolley beds, patients – the walking wounded, the drunks – either pace the floors like hyped-up zombies or sit slumped in chairs.

The exit sign is at the end of the corridor. *Way Out. Car Park and Eastern Road.* I walk towards it – not too fast, don't want to attract attention. As I step on a black rubber mat the door automatically swings open. I turn around, checking that no one has clocked me, that no one is calling security, raising alarms.

That's when I see them.

The handsome doctor with the weird skin is at the reception desk talking to two women – one with frizzy hair and a long flowing coat, the other with a dark suit and short hair and priestly collar at her neck.

Missy.

Reverend Anne.

What are they doing here? Together?

Through the open door I feel the salty chill of sea air on my face.

Go, I think. *Before they catch you. Forget about Missy. Forget about the school, that doctor, Reverend Anne. Looking for your friend – just think about that. Finding Hannah – that's all that matters ...*

I sit on the bus shelter bench, shivering. The light khaki jacket I threw over my T-shirt and jeans when I left school in the morning isn't enough to keep out the wind and rain that's blowing up off the seafront tonight. Four old ladies in padded jackets and see-through perm protectors huddle in the shelter, too. They've just come out of the bingo hall across the road. They're puffing away on cigarettes, telling each other jokes, cackling like hags.

I feel something in the pocket of my jeans. It's my phone – trembling and shaking like a grenade about to explode. With numb fingers, I check the screen. Private number – could it be Hannah? Or is it Missy or Reverend Anne, trying to track me down?

I slide the screen to answer. The ringing stops.

'Maddy?'

My heart catches in my throat. Hannah's voice – it's her!

'Yes, it's me!' My mind's racing so fast I can hardly get the words out. 'It's Maddy.'

'Maddy, you've got to listen to me, carefully. I'm in the . . .'

A car rattles by. I turn my back to the road, put the phone closer to my ear.

'I can't hear you, Hannah. What did you say?'

The bus turns in to the stop. The door screeches open, the four ladies get in.

'I'm in the . . .'

The bus engine roars as it pulls away, gears grinding.

'What, Hannah? I didn't hear you.

I wait for her to answer, but there's only static and echoing sounds, as if she's dropped the phone.

Somebody screams.

'Hannah? Where are you?'

Nothing. More static, and then silence.

I try to find the number, but there's no record on my phone. I stare at the screen, willing a text to appear.

The road finally goes quiet, as the old ladies' bus gets smaller and smaller. I slump back down on the plastic bench. It reminds me of Hannah and I missing the bus back to the school Saturday night and having to walk through the –

Woods? Is that what Hannah was trying to say?

'I'm in the –'

Is that the missing word – *woods*?

Hannah's words in the jumbled up voicemail. *Dark. Trees.*

That must be it! My heart races with fear when I remember those pictures in the book – the clearing and the fire in the depths of forest. Does somebody have Hannah? Is she being held against her will in the only place she's ever been frightened – Crowham Wood?

26

The Brighton police waiting room is like a quieter, grubbier version of Sussex A & E. A woman leafs through a tatty magazine full of stories and pictures of already-forgotten celebrities, while I struggle to stay awake.

An officer in uniform steps up to the reception counter and motions for me. He's beefy and red-faced, with baggy eyes that make it look like he hasn't slept for weeks. He reads what I've written down, mutters *okay* a few times, nods.

'You want to report a missing person?'

'Yes, please.'

He reads some more. 'Hannah Masupha-Harris. Crowham Martyrs School . . . We'd expect to have heard from the school if one of their pupils had gone missing.'

'It's because they're lying about it.'

The officer looks at me, raising his eyebrows. 'Lying?'

I take a deep breath – I can't panic, mustn't sound crazy. 'They're spreading some story about Hannah going off with her

159

aunt, but she doesn't *have* an aunt, at least not in this country, and there's no –'

The officer puts his hand up so I'll stop talking, and nods his head slowly, as if he's trying to calm me down. 'And when was the last time *you* had contact with your friend, young lady?'

'She just called me.'

The officer puts down his clipboard. 'So why do you think she's in trouble?'

'Because I heard screaming. And other weird noises on the phone. And then the line went totally dead.'

I reach into my pocket for my phone. 'She left a voicemail yesterday, too.'

I'm about to punch in my voicemail number so the officer can listen to the message, but something's not right. My phone's screen is lit up, shiny and blue, but it's completely blank – there are no apps, no contacts, no games.

'Everything's g-gone,' I stammer.

I show him the phone, as if that will prove I'm not lying.

'Maybe you've been hacked,' he says.

Is he joking? I can't tell. I turn the phone off and on. Still nothing.

'But there were three messages,' I say, my eyes filling with tears. 'One was from my mum, and one was from Hannah – I just listened to it before I came here and she said something about it being dark and something about trees –'

'Trees?'

I take a deep breath. I have to sound normal, sane – I have to make sense.

'I think they've taken her to Crowham Wood.'

The officer looks down at his clipboard again. He ticks a few things with his pen, draws some circles. 'The forest next to the school?'

I nod. Finally, I think. Finally, I'm getting somewhere.

'I'll tell you what,' the policeman says. 'Crowham Wood isn't in our jurisdiction, but I'll put this through and see what we can come up with.'

'Thank you,' I gush. Tears of relief spring to my eyes. 'Thank you so much.'

The officer nods at the seats. 'You wait there. I'll make a few phone calls and see if we can get this sorted.'

I'm slumped in the back of the police car, trying desperately to stay awake. What time is it? It must be after midnight.

The rain comes down in sheets, covering the window like a clear river of melted plastic, so it's all a blur. We're on the A23 –

I recognise the bright lights of Tesco and the BP station – and as soon as the car turns off the dual carriageway and the road starts twisting and turning through the South Downs, I know where we're headed.

It's not Crowham Wood.

It's not the Royal Sussex Hospital, either.

The car slows as we reach the school gates. How could I have been so stupid? How could I have trusted him?

I close my eyes, listen to the slap of the windscreen wipers, the squawks and crackles of the police radio. I straighten my back, run my hand along the door. If I could find the handle maybe I could jump out.

'Can't we take a look in the woods?'

Nobody answers. Not the baggy-eyed cop who's driving, not the female youth liaison officer.

'She's there, I know it.'

Not a word. I'm not only invisible, I don't even exist.

'Please,' I say. 'Have a look. It won't take long, I promise.'

The car stops. The front doors open, the female officer comes around to my side. I get out slowly, and when she steps back I take off running down the gravel path, towards the gates, the woods –

'Stop, Maddy!'

Their footsteps crunch behind me.

'All right, young lady, that's it.'

The female officer's got me around the waist. She's picking me up, swinging me.

'We've had just about enough of this –'

I kick her in the shins as she drags me up the path. I pull at the hands that are clenched tight around my body.

'This school is full of liars!' I shout. 'Hannah's been kidnapped – she's in the woods –'

The front door opens. Missy steps outside, still in the long coat I saw her wearing at the hospital. The policeman rushes up the path, helps haul me in. I try to kick him away, but he's stronger than me too. Like an animal, I'm half-carried, half-dragged towards the front door.

'Wake up, everybody,' I shout. 'Hannah's been abducted!'

The junior boys' dormitory is at the front of the building. Somebody's bound to crawl out of bed, go the window to see what all the excitement is.

'Jordan! Darshan! You've got to help me find Hannah!'

Before I can say anything more I'm bundled into the entrance hall and the door is closed and locked.

Missy stands between Mr Casey and Mrs Gibson, her arms crossed.

'Thank you so much, officers,' she sighs. 'Maddy's been under such a strain the past few months. First she started having seizures like the one she had today, and then her best friend moved back to South Africa –'

What?

'She's lying,' I say. 'Hannah didn't move anywhere. Hannah's in the woods. I talked to her tonight. Somebody's taken her – I heard her scream.'

Mrs Gibson takes my arm, digs her fingers in a bit, pulls me across the floor. She's still wearing her cook's uniform from dinner, still smells of fried onions and chicken gravy. When I stumble on the edge of the carpet she stops, pulls me back up, gives the side of my face a little slap.

'You stop this right now,' she hisses.

'Hey!' I shriek. 'Did you see that?'

The police officers are in the doorway, backs turned. They're talking to Mr Casey and Missy – are they in on it, too?

'Help! I shout. 'Anybody!'

I feel that weird energy again – what I felt with Caleb – but it's inside my body, like pure adrenaline rushing through my veins.

Mrs Gibson claws my arms again, but I this time I can't feel a thing.

'Ouch,' she shrieks, and I hear a crack as one of her fingernails breaks. 'What are you doing, you little –'

'I'm doing nothing,' I say. 'You're the one who's hurting me.'

'She's messing me about,' Mrs Gibson shouts. 'Playing some trick.'

Mr Casey runs towards me as Missy bolts the front door. Mrs Gibson is still sucking on her fingers, blowing on the nails.

'I told you this would happen,' she growls.

Mr Casey grabs my arms, pins them to the side of my body.

'Sorry about this,' he whispers. 'Really sorry, but it's for your own –'

'Hey!' I kick and shout out as he shoves me towards the door to the admin corridor, but it's no use. He pushes the door open and someone behind us reaches into my pockets – they're taking my phone! I try to scream again, but something's being shoved into my mouth, forcing it open, pushing my tongue to the back of my throat.

I try to kick again, but the gag is making me dizzy and weak.

The jostling stops for a second and I feel hands on my neck, my head, as something soft is –

Everything goes dark, only this time I'm awake. As the hood is slipped over my head, I know the nightmare is real.

27

'This is not what it looks like,' Mr Casey says.

'First you stole my mobile, then I was bundled down to a room in the basement with a hood over my head and a gag in my mouth. There's a single light hanging from the ceiling, and I'm squashed behind a massive table so I can't move.'

Mr Casey looks at the floor. Missy digs something out of her bag – a tiny spiral-bound notebook. Only Mrs Gibson's got the *cajones* to actually look at me.

I stare right back at her, remembering what Hannah said about not showing them we're scared. 'How could this look like anything bad?'

'It's for your own good,' Mr Casey mumbles, but even he doesn't sound convinced. 'You've got to listen to them.'

Mrs Gibson coughs.

'To *us*, I mean. All of us.'

Mrs Gibson finds a tissue in her pocket. She wipes sweat off her forehead, and pushes a lock of dull grey hair. When Missy clicks her handbag shut, the sound echoes round the room like the ricochet of a tiny bullet.

'Right.' Mr Casey fiddles with the pen in his hand. 'I guess we should get started.'

'Stop all this "we" stuff, okay? I'm not part of your creepy little gang, so the sooner *I* get out of here, the happier *I'll* be.'

'You won't be –'

'Why don't you ring my mum in LA?' I push against the table, but it seems to be locked into place. 'If you're so desperate to get rid of me why don't you call her on my phone right now and tell her I've done something bad and been expelled. That I'm on my way to Gatwick – she can book me a flight.'

I give the desk another push. Nothing.

'You won't be going home, Maddy. It's safer here.'

'Safer? You call this *safe?*'

It's all like something out of a movie – so ridiculous and freaky, that I have to laugh.

'Stop it, Maddy,' Missy says. 'This is serious.'

'No,' I say. 'It's pathetic. Just tell me where Hannah is and –'

'You have no idea how much trouble you're in.'

'Me? I'm in trouble? My mum lives in Los Angeles, the lawsuit capital of the known universe. Her boyfriend's completely loaded, and by the time his lawyers are finished with you –'

Ghosts arrive, looking like illuminated lava-lamp clumps. The silvery, shimmery one is here. She pulls away from the heavy cluster and does her own swirly dance behind Mrs Gibson's head, while her lumpy mates drop to the floor, hide behind the stacks of broken furniture like terrified children.

'Did you hear me, Maddy? Are you listening?'

Children – is that what the ghosts at Crowham are? I always wondered . . .

'Maddy, please.'

It makes sense, in a twisted sort of way. The people who used to run the school – the priests or monks, or whoever they were – were they murderers? Child killers? Was the school a trap, a way to lure in children whose parents were dead or couldn't care for them? Is that why there are so many ghosts here?

'Maddy, you've got to listen to us.'

Is it *still* a trap? The underground room, the dark tunnels – is this some kind of torture chamber?

I bang on the table, look up at the ceiling. 'Hey!'

'Stop that,' Mr Casey says.

I do it again, as loud and as hard as I can. 'Anybody. Help me!'

I shout and bang until my hand hurts and my voice strains and scratches.

'Maddy, they'll hear you.'

'That's what I *want*, you stupid –'

'NO!' Mrs Gibson lurches across the table, grabs my wrists with huge hands that grip like steel claws.

'Please, Maddy,' Missy whispers. 'Just be quiet and listen. You have to listen or –'

'Or what?' I try to squirm out of Mrs Gibson's cuffs, but it's pointless. 'You'll cut down on my dinner portions? Make me eat lumpy porridge for breakfast?' Mrs Gibson leans across the table, close enough so that I could spit at her if I wanted to, or bite off a chunk of her nose –

'Or something terrible will happen,' Missy says.

'More terrible than this?'

Mrs Gibson lets go and leans back again, adjusting her tabard. 'You've no idea,' she whispers.

'Andrew, tell her,' Missy rasps.

Mr Casey pushes his chair back and stands up.

'Right,' he says. 'This may sound a bit strange.'

He stands up, walks in a little circle, like when he's teaching – away from the table, then back. I half expect a screen to lower down from the ceiling so he can use one of his slideshows.

He looks at Missy.

'Look, Betty – Miss Burke – could we move the table first? The poor kid can hardly breathe.'

Missy shakes her head. She's not taking any chances.

'Right then. I'll make this quick.' Mr Casey takes a big breath. 'Many years ago. Many *hundreds* of years ago . . .'

Mrs Gibson coughs, rustles her chair so the rubber ends on the legs squeak.

'All right, *thousands*.'

He stops, shakes his head, sighs, tries another angle. 'You know the school is called the Crowham Martyrs? Well, everyone assumes that the martyrs were killed for their religious beliefs. And that's fine. It's good that people think that. But . . .'

He pauses for a moment. Mrs Gibson coughs again – a not very subtle hint that he should get a move on.

'But the Crowham Martyrs who were murdered and burned like animals weren't tortured or killed because of their faith. They weren't Catholic nuns, like it says in the official history of the school, Maddy. In fact, you won't read about the Martyrs in any history book because . . .'

Mr Casey pauses and looks over at Missy and Mrs Gibson as if he's waiting for permission to continue. I think of the sounds – the wailing and weeping, the crackling flames.

'They were witches, Maddy.'

Missy leans in a little, watching my face. Mrs Gibson takes out the grimy tissues, gives her skin another wipe down.

'*Real* witches, with real powers of magic. Good powers, but *real* powers.'

170

My heart flutters. Why are they telling me this? It can't be true, no matter what crazy things I've imagined.

'They lived here in the old convent. Had done for centuries, even before the original building was built, long before Christianity was heard of, and they kept the place safe.'

That word again. *Safe.*

'From what?' I say, trying to keep my voice steady. 'Ofsted inspectors? Kids in hoodies?' I sneer at him. 'From *you*?'

'From demons,' Mr Casey says.

'From the devil who burned them,' Mrs Gibson says.

Missy waits a few seconds before speaking. 'From the unimaginable forces of evil who live in Crowham Wood.'

I have to stay calm. Blank. This is a trap – a terrible trick to get me to talk – but I can't let them know anything about the ghosts or the books that Hannah and I found in that library.

'You know they're here, Maddy.'

I shake my head. *Badness.* That was just Hannah's imagination – Reverend Anne said as much when she talked about Tokoloshe. And Jordan saw *fings* because he was scared.

'You can see them.'

I shake my head. They are *not* what I see. Demons are just in books, only in pictures –

'You *can*, Maddy –'

171

'I can't.' I bang my fists on the table, and the whole room seems to shake.

'Jordan can.'

I stop pounding. Okay. So Jordan must have told them about the *fings* and they believed him. He must have told them about the scary man he thought he saw.

'And what about your friend Hannah?'

'That's what I'd like to know.'

'You both felt those demons, Maddy, when you walked through the woods.'

Finally, I raise my face and look across the table at them. I try to read their expressions. Blank. Still. Calm. Not afraid, not angry, not even nasty – just, nothing.

And that's how I feel, too – empty and hollow.

'Have you been spying on us?' I say. 'Following us? Listening in on our conversations? Are you the ones who hacked my phone and wiped Hannah's message?'

No one answers me. I slump down in my chair, listening for sounds outside this room – there must be something normal that I can hear – birds singing, a radio playing, alarm bells, it doesn't matter.

'Can we stop all this, please?' I say. 'There's no such thing as witches or demons.'

'There's no such things as ghosts, either,' Missy says.

My heart pulls and my hollowed-out stomach twists.

Say nothing, I think. *Stay still. Be a statue. Face of stone.*

'We know all about you and the ghosts, Maddy.'

If I blank them out maybe they'll think they've got it all wrong, maybe they'll realise that there's nothing special about me.

'We've always known, since before you arrived.'

What? But how can that be true? Mum told me never, ever to tell. It was a secret – *our* secret.

'We know all about you, Maddy . . .'

I look down at the table. There are words etched in the dull metal. Maybe it's a clue, or message from Hannah. I tune out what Missy's saying and rub the words to see if that makes them clearer. When I turn my head sideways I see letters that are square and old-fashioned, like the letters in the books, like the words on my computer screen.

. . . cruelties . . .

Missy's voice is a fuzzy drone in the background, another set of words that I don't understand.

. . . the infernal . . .

'Can you hear me, Maddy?'

. . . the fiend himself . . .

Missy worms her way back into my hearing.

'Are you listening?'

The written words fade and disappear. I look up from the table.

'What I said about your mother?'

I shake my head. No, I didn't hear what she said. And no, I don't *want* to hear.

'There's nothing to say.' The words scratch my parched throat.

'So you understand that it's all for your own good, Maddy?' She waves her arms around the room, raises them to the ceiling. 'All of this.'

'Kidnapping my best friend – how is that good?'

'Hannah is safe, Maddy,' Missy says. 'We already told you.'

'And holding me captive in some dungeon, what's good about that?'

I push the table again.

'But didn't you hear me? It's what your mother wanted –'

'You don't know *anything* about my mother, you nasty old –'

'You need to stay calm, Maddy. You mustn't get angry.'

Mr Casey is on his feet.

'You have to listen to what we're trying to tell you, Maddy,' he says. 'You have to stay put from now on – no more running away – and in the morning you can get back to lessons and forget all about this.'

'Are you crazy?' I ask.

'And if anything strange happens –'

'Stranger than *this?*'

I shove against the table, as hard as I can, so hard it hurts my hands and ribs and stomach, until I get a sudden rush of strength and the table moves, taking off as if it's got a life of its own, careering across the floor so fast that Missy and Mrs Gibson have to move out of the way.

They shout something to Mr Casey, but I can't hear the words because I'm on my feet and when I get to the door I bang on it, grappling for the handle, turning it, shoving the door with my hip so it opens and I fly through.

Down the corridor. Safety lamps covered with rusty wire. Wet, dripping walls. I can hardly see but I keep going because I don't care where this leads – to the other side of the school, to the other side of the world, to China, to hell – to anywhere, but here.

I stumble through the near-darkness, not daring to stop and look behind me, not knowing if I'm running away from danger or towards it. My feet stir up fragments of old cinder, and tiny bits of ashy grit fill up my lungs, making it hard to breathe. The ghosts are here too, as thick and wet as fog out on the ocean. As I cut through them, their coldness tingles on my skin and an icy chill cools my burning lungs.

Finally, I see light. It's coming from a narrow window well. A small pane of grimy glass lets in a dull orb of light from the outside – the main entrance must be above me, so that's the security light filtering into this dungeon.

There are stacks of boxes beside the window. I want to slump down between them, stay hidden for as long as I can, sleep until somebody nudges me awake and . . .

No. I have to get out of here. I have to find Hannah. I have to call Mum, so she can book flights, help Hannah and me get away from this horrible place.

I look up at the window. What if I used the boxes to make a tower? I grab the thick leather handle of one of the crates, heave and pull with all my might. It shifts easily enough, and I pull another one over, then another. Within a few minutes I have two levels of a pyramid. All I need is one more box and I'll be able to clamber to the top, reach the window, either open it or smash the glass, and climb out.

The next box doesn't move. I pull on the handle, shove it with my legs, but it won't budge. I try the one next to it – just as heavy. I go to the next, hold on to the side handles of heavy rope, take a deep breath and bend my legs like a power lifter – nothing!

The entire row of crates – all too heavy. So what can I do? I'll have to open them, take out whatever's inside.

I sit down on the last crate. It's dark here, so far away from the window well. A ghost swooshes around the box, searching for a way in. I can hardly see, so I don't know if the ghost is the pretty one – I can only tell it's there from the feeling of coldness, the slight sound like rustling silk.

And when it disappears under the box's coffin-like lid it hits me.

Ghosts. A crypt-like basement. A missing friend. A school run by lunatics and liars. Books of devil pictures. Dust-covered crates – full of what? What?

I smell it first. A horrible stench seeps out from under the lid. And then I see what's inside – at least I think I do – even when I look away.

Bodies. Rotting corpses. Bones.

I try not to cry – I mustn't, in case someone hears me – and for a few seconds I manage to keep my feelings locked inside until finally my face crumples, my throat constricts, tears run down my cheeks, and I can't stop the horrible, choking sobs that rise up from deep inside me.

I sink to the floor, tuck my head to my knees, imagining those skeletons wearing the heavy chains they were brought here in. For how many years, I wonder? Witches, Catholics, Protestants, priests, nuns, children, anybody who got in the way of –

What? That's what I don't understand – got in the way of what? Who?

I wish I knew. If only I understood what I was really up against, then I could –

Hannah. Is this where they've put her? Is she inside one of these boxes, rotting away with all the others?

I hear footsteps coming, but I don't even try to cover my sobs. As they get closer all I can think is *good* – whoever it is, let them find me. What can they do – Missy, Mr Casey, the ghosts, the others – the *fings*, whoever, whatever they are?

Can they kill me?

Fine. I'd rather be dead.

Can they send me to hell?

Too late, I'll tell them. I'm already here.

29

The coughing gives him away.

Too much dust again, filling Mr Casey's asthmatic lungs. He shouldn't be down here, the idiot. Serves him right if he –

'Maddy!'

He coughs even harder.

'Maddy, I know you're here.'

Fine, I think. Know all you want.

The ghost slips out from inside the box. Shimmers in a dull glow that reaches my hiding place. She swirls around, circling my feet.

'Maddy, you're being silly. It's time you understood everything – you're old enough, I'm sure you can handle it.'

He sighs.

'It's time to tell you the truth.'

I curl up more tightly. Put my fingers in my ears. *The truth*, I think, *yeah right*.

'I know you can hear me so I'm going to keep talking.'

I try to block out his voice the way I did Missy's. I think of good things – me and Mum driving up the coastal highway to Big Sur, shrieking along to the songs on the radio –

'You were brought to Crowham by people who care about you.'

Remember a song, Maddy, hum along in your head.

'Maddy, did you hear me? People who *love* you.'

Who? I want to shriek. Who loves me here? No one. Nobody loves me – except for Mum and she's not here. My mum loves me – she's the only one. The only person in the world.

I scrunch myself up even further. Squeeze my eyes shut, so I'm in darkness . . . 'People like Miss Burke, Maddy, and they are trying to protect you.'

I can't help it. My guard's let down by so many lies – I'm like a boxer who doesn't have the strength to defend herself any more.

'That's rubbish,' I shout.

My words bounce around the walls, seem to stir up more dust.

'Locking me up, holding me hostage – is that how they take care of me?'

'Yes, Maddy. That is how we are keeping you safe.'

He's shouting, too, even though he's coughing every other word.

'Miss Burke is not what she seems, Maddy – none of us are.'

'You think I don't know that? You think I can't tell that you're all a bunch of –'

'Miss Burke.' Mr Casey gasps. 'She's –'

'A witch,' I shriek. 'That's what she is. An evil, bloody, ugly –

'Stop shouting, Maddy!'

Something near me shakes, as if whatever's inside these boxes has come to life.

'Witch!' I'm screaming at the top of my lungs – louder than any noise I've ever made. 'WITCHWITCHWITCH!'

I'm on my feet, blazing with anger, jumping up and down, stomping the ground and shaking my fists, shrieking the words until my vocal cords feel like they're being ripped to shreds.

When I finally stop, the ground rumbles – a weird aftershock – and then it's quiet. Almost silent, except for a low moan. Not a witchy, imagined one, but the real groan of a human being in pain.

'Mr Casey?'

A slight cough in the darkness.

'Are you there, Sir?'

Another cough, even fainter.

Then the sound of wheezing, someone struggling for breath.

Mr Casey!

I tiptoe closer, straining to hear, my throat still on fire, my ears clogged with pain.

I crouch on to the ground and scuttle on all fours, scratching the floor in front of me like a blind rat.

'Maddy.' A low croak.

Finally, I'm close enough to see him, curled up on the floor. 'I'm here, Sir,' I whisper.

'My back pocket,' he groans.

I turn him on to his side, reach in his pocket. I take out a thin leather wallet, a set of keys, his mobile.

I hold each one up for him but he shakes his head.

I reach in again, find his inhaler.

'Got it, Sir.'

I click the lid, hold it to his mouth. He takes in a raspy breath – not nearly enough.

'Come on,' I say. 'Try again, Sir.'

He shakes his head. Scraggy curls, like a sheepdog's fur, cover his face.

'Too late,' he whispers. 'No time.'

'No, Sir, don't say that.' I pick up the phone, and as I turn it on the screen lights up. 'I'll call 999.'

He shakes his head. 'He. He's . . .'

A single bar of signal.

'Got it,' I say, my hands trembling.

I key in the numbers, but the signal's lost so I turn the screen, and the light hits Mr Casey's face. His skin has gone purple and his eyes bulge out as if somebody's got their fingers around his neck.'

'Hang on, Sir,' I whisper.

The signal bar appears again. I key in the numbers, but nothing happens. I try again, but my hands shake so hard I can hardly hang on to the phone.

Mr Casey coughs. 'It's too late . . .'

'It's not, Sir . . .'

The phone clatters to the floor, as if it's been snatched from my hands.

'Your mother,' Mr Casey gasps.

I steady my hands, scrabble around on the ground for the phone.

'Your mother isn't . . .'

He runs out of breath, of voice.

'What are you saying, Sir?' I whisper. 'My mother isn't what?'

Mr Casey gestures for me to move closer. His eyes are wide with terror, his face goes from purple to white, all colour gone, but he manages to turn his head, stare into the darkness as if he's looking for something. His pale lips tremble . . .

'Your father . . . He is . . .'

'Sir?' I whisper.

When he turns back to me, his eyes have changed. They're round black mirrors, reflecting what seem to be another pair of dark, glowing eyes.

'Mr Casey?'

His head twists violently, as if someone has grabbed it. I hear a horrible grunt, as air is forced from his lungs.

I wait for him to take another breath . . .

'Sir?'

I jostle him on the shoulder. No movement. No breathing. 'Wake up, Sir,' I whisper. 'Wake up.'

I shake him again.

Nothing.

I shake him and shake him but he never wakes up.

30

I'm back in my hiding place beside the crates.

Did I faint again? Did I sleep? How long have I been here?

From where I'm cowering I can see the outline of Mr Casey's body. It's a smudge on the edge of the dim light – like an abstract painting, black on grey.

So nobody followed us or came looking. So nobody's called for an ambulance to take him away.

So nobody knows.

Sir's mobile is lying on the floor a few feet away, where it landed when it flew out of my hands. I reach over to pick it up. The light comes on and I can see how badly it cracked when crashed to the floor. It seems to be working, though – the clock says that it's 5.45 a.m. – so I dial 999.

Nothing. No signal here in the darkest corner of the bottom of the building.

I wrap my arms around my head and hunker down. I need to think. It's too late to help him, but maybe I can come up with a plan to get out of here now that it's morning; to tell someone, to escape, find Hannah, maybe take Jordan and Darshan away, too, before someone – some *fing* – comes for them, as well.

Oh, Mr Casey. Poor, poor Sir.

I've never seen anyone die. Every day, all those ghosts, those legions of the dead, but this . . .

I should go back to the church and tell Reverend Anne what's happened. Maybe right now she's kneeling in front of the St Michael statue. Maybe she's lighting a candle, saying a prayer to the Archangel and Protector.

I look over at Mr Casey. No prayers in this place. None for him, none for me.

Alone in the dark. No candles. No angel.

I crawl on my knees, inching closer to where he's lying. I try 999 again, but there's still no signal, still no help for poor Sir. At least the phone's something to cling on to, a dim source of light.

I shuffle randomly through the contact names, as if that might take my mind off what's happened to him.

Fergusson, Healy, Kay, Lee...

Who are these people? Sisters or brothers? Cousins? Friends? Will they miss Mr Casey? Will they be at his funeral? Will they cry for him?

I scroll back.

Elizabeth B

I know who that is – Missy.

I glance at the other names.

Monica, Pannett, Valelly

Rev A – I know who that is, too.

Susannah

Susannah. That's Mum's name.

I check the number.

Mum's phone in America. Why would Mr Casey have that?

Your mother isn't . . .

Mr Casey must know her. But how? Why?

It doesn't matter now, does it?

Your father . . . He is . . .

What would he know about my father? Nothing. How could he, when even I don't? He was just rambling. Delirious.

I hear noises – grinding and clanking, like a distant army in chains. I try to shake them out of my head as I crawl closer to Mr Casey's body.

'God bless you, Sir,' I whisper.

I touch the lids of his eyes – reflecting nothing now except the dim yellow light – and close them one at a time.

The light from Sir's phone catches something I hadn't noticed before – smudges on the dusty floor. I shine the light closer. What are they? Footprints? They don't look like human feet, they're more like man-sized claws. Maybe they're animal tracks. Weird that they'd be here in the basement, though, and that they'd be so –

Claws?

I fumble for the off button on Sir's phone and scoot back to my hiding place. I remember that night in the forest. That horrible growling – what was that? And those deep slashes on the windows in the village. Are these the same?

No, no. I huddle in the shadows, trembling, cradling Mr Casey's phone. It's better here, not moving, not breathing, just waiting – silently, invisibly – for my fear to subside.

But the distant noises get louder. They creep closer and closer until they hit me like a thunderclap of groaning and grinding and screaming. I drag myself out of the darkness – no choice but to run – as the vibrations smash into me, hurtling my body forward into the darkness.

As I race away from the sound, Mr Casey's phone clatters on to the floor. Something's behind me – I feel it breathing on my neck, scratching me with needle-sharp talons – getting closer now, close enough to kill me if I stumble, to cut me to pieces or grab my throat until . . .

In front of me something glows, like a fading torchlight. It's a ghost – the pretty one, my almost-invisible friend. Blindly, I follow, not daring to take my eyes off the swirling glimmer. Those tiny gaps, I think – the cracks she can slip into and under with such ease, such grace. Maybe she'll find a space big enough for me to fit through.

A stronger light appears ahead of the ghost – a narrow strip, like a blade of brightness above my head. As I get closer, it seeps into the darkness, illuminating something that's solid, wooden.

A staircase! And at the top of it, a door! The ghost hovers in front of me and then slips under, into the light.

I clamber up the steps.

When I get to the top, the noises below me go quiet. What are they doing? Waiting for me to tumble back down? Regrouping before a final attack?

I turn around and look. A thick blanket of ghosts hovers between me and the bottom of the stairs. It's as if they're helping me – Hannah was right – forming a barricade, keeping those invisible *fings* at bay. And what's on the other side of the door?

Footsteps – human ones – shuffle across a hard floor. Pots are clanging, glass is tinkling. I smell things, too – grilled bacon, burnt toast. These are the sounds and smells of breakfast – it's morning and I'm outside a door that leads to the kitchen!

Behind me, the sounds get louder again.

'Help!' I shout. 'I'm locked in the basement.'

I put my fist to the door, ready to pound it again. Then I remember – Mrs Gibson's the head cook – what would happen if *she* opened the door? She'd probably push me down the stairs, hoping I'd break my neck and lie undiscovered in the basement, rotting away with Mr Casey until the worms had done their worst and she could shove me into a crate with –

No. Don't think of it, Maddy.

I hunker on the top stair, leaning against the door, grateful for the narrow strip of light, but frightened of what it leads to.

On the other side, I hear music. Someone who's far too chirpy to be Mrs Gibson is singing. One of the dinner ladies – a nice one, I hope. A smiler.

I knock quietly. 'Hello?'

Something clatters to the floor – a metal pot, a saucepan lid.

'It's me . . . Maddy. Maddy Deeprose.'

'Maddy? What are you doing in there?'

'I came back from hospital in the middle of the night and I took the wrong staircase by mistake and –

'Mrs Gibson isn't here right now.'

'That's okay,' I say. 'You can let me in, can't you? There must be a key.'

'There's one in the lock, but I don't think Mrs Gibson would want me –'

'Please,' I say. 'It's cold down here.'

The noises below me begin again, grow louder. The ghost barricade is shifting, struggling to stay together, thinning in places.

'It's scary, too.'

It takes her a moment to open it – she grunts and groans and mutters about having to get the caretaker to have a look.

Finally the key turns, the door opens, and I tumble out into a world of brightness and warmth.

'I always wondered what was behind that door.'

The dinner lady peers into the darkness. 'Oh, I don't like the look of that basement at all.' She locks the door and looks at me – trembling and dizzy – her eyes furrowed with worry.

'You all right, love?'

I think about Mr Casey, down there on his own. I need to tell her that he's dead – I *have* to tell her – but when I open my mouth the words don't come. I try to speak, but the grinding noises are still in my head – low and growly like a dog that's willing to bide his time – and all that comes out is a grunt.

'What are you trying to say, dear?'

I'm still shaking, stuttering, struggling to get the words out. 'Mr . . . S-Sir . . .'

'It's all right, pet, just take your time.'

I speak slowly, taking a deep breath between each syllable. 'Mis-ter. C-Casey . . .'

'What about him?'

'He's d-down there . . .'

I point to the door, and my whole arm shakes. I think about

all those years ago, what Mum said about the ghosts, about *never, ever* telling. Is this what she was afraid of? That I'd choke to death, like Mr Casey? But this is so much worse than the ghosts, this is something –

The dinner lady's reaching into her pocket, taking out her mobile.

'He's d-dead,' I say, before staggering out of the kitchen, and stumbling away as fast as I can.

My bedroom's been trashed.

Clothes and papers litter the floor. I check the wardrobe – my dirty laundry's still there, but the hidden devil books are gone.

Is that what they were looking for? Then why has everything else been wrecked, too? My pictures of me and Mum are face down on the ground, their frames smashed. I tiptoe across the carpet and pick up them up, carefully taking them out of the frames and blowing away the fragments of glass. Then I take out the rucksack that's under my bed and zip the pictures into the outside pocket.

I fill the main part with clothes from the floor – dirty or clean, I don't care – and knickers and socks from the dresser that's been pulled away from the wall.

I need to get out, before the other students wake up, before the dinner lady tells Missy and Mrs Gibson, before –

Mr Casey's contorted, purple face.

Poor Sir. All alone in that horrible basement . . .

But at least I've told someone. At least he'll soon be out of there and on his way to –

Poor, poor Sir.

I go to my overturned desk, pull out the drawers. My passport – where is it? I can't get to LA without it – where has it gone?

I sift through the sea of scattered paper – it's not there, and neither is my debit card. I look again, rifling through everything, turning over the bin, checking under the mattress, behind the wardrobe, as my thoughts swirl and swim in panic.

Nothing.

Am I trapped now? Stuck in this place with no hope of ever getting home?

Just think, Maddy. You can get a new passport at a post office. It'll be easy, right? You can go back to town, find a way to get in touch with Mum. She'll sort everything out from LA.

She must know somebody in London who can help, who can lend me money and get me a new passport and –

Footsteps on the staircase. I go to the door, turn the key to lock it.

Then I head for my bathroom – toothbrush, soap, spot cream – everything's swept into the bag.

The handle jiggles as somebody pulls and tugs at the door to my room. There's a hard shove, and I hold my breath, waiting for it to be smashed down by an enormous monster or shredded to bits by an animal's claws.

But the noise stops and a few seconds later the key falls to the floor with a gentle tink. I pull the bathroom door until it's almost shut. I lean against the wall, and crane my neck so that I can peer through the gap into my room.

The lock clicks, and my bedroom door creaks open.

Caleb creeps in, looking like he's just got out of bed – wearing pyjama bottoms and a T-shirt, his hair sticking out in crazy spirals.

He checks the staircase, closes the door.

I lose sight of him when he steps into the room, but it sounds like he's searching through my stuff – why would he do that? What could he want? Those devil books he was so interested in?

I inch closer to the door, trying to see out the gap, but suddenly the hinges squeak and the door swings open and Caleb is standing in front of me.

'God, Maddy, what are you playing at?'

He takes me roughly by the arm, drags me into the bedroom.

'What am *I* playing at?' I pull away from him, rubbing my shoulder. 'You have no right to be here, no right to poke around in my things.'

'Shhh.'

Another set of footsteps climbs the stairs.

'Quick. In the bathroom.'

Caleb pushes me in front of him and closes the door. Through the narrow gap between the door and the frame I can see Missy step in. She looks around, nods appreciatively at the mess, then backs away again.

'You know you can't leave,' Caleb says.

He's standing close to me, his breath is warm on my face. For a moment I wait for the pulse, the pull, but then I push past him into the bedroom and he follows me, carrying my rucksack.

'Not now, Maddy. It's not safe.'

I rush to the door. *Safe,* I think. *Don't make me laugh.*

My heart's pounding, a bead of sweat trickles down my brow. I need to get away. I need to break out of this room, this school, before they can find me and drag me back down to that basement.

Caleb's already in front of me, blocking my way.

'Please, Maddy.'

I back off, turn around. The window – I'll try that.

'You've got to trust me.'

As he grabs me from behind and holds me close to him, I struggle to break free – kicking, clawing at the hands that are tightening around mine.

'You need to calm down, Maddy – to listen.'

I squirm again, try a back-kick to the shins –

'Ouch!' Caleb loosens his hold and I scramble towards the door, but he grabs my arm, hauls me back.

'I only came to Crowham so I could help you,' he says. His voice is like warm honey, but my wrist hurts where he's holding me, and I think of those dreams – the screams, the pain.

'Help me?' I blub. 'By creeping about in my room and going through my stuff? And right after my friend's been kidnapped?'

'Come on, Maddy,' he sighs, letting go of my wrist, 'nobody kidnapped Hannah.'

'What about Mr Casey?' I spit. 'I suppose he's not dead either.'

He shakes his head. 'What?'

'Did they trick him into going to the basement? Did they make him chase me until his lungs were clogged up and he couldn't breathe?'

Suddenly I can't take any more. I think of Mr Casey's twisted face, his struggle to speak, the reflection on his eyes. I remember all the noises, and the hot breath on my neck –

My whole body shakes and shudders – I feel dizzy and faint.

'Maddy? You've got to tell me what you mean. Who's *they*?

I lower myself to the floor. I hug my knees and rock back

and forth, remembering Mr Casey in that basement.

'Poor Sir,' I say, over and over. 'Poor Sir, poor Sir, poor Sir.'

Caleb sits beside me. He puts his arm around my shoulder – I don't have the power to push him away. Again, I wait for the electricity – the charge, the pulse. But there's nothing between us, just prickly sweat that soaks through my clothes, and the gritty dirt ground into my skin.

'I already told you,' I sob. 'Sir's in the basement. Dead.'

Caleb doesn't answer. He waits while I cry it all out, until I can breathe normally, until I wipe the tears from my face with the sleeve of my T-shirt.

When I'm quiet, he finally speaks.

'Maddy, this school is a strange place.'

'You think?' I say, and I break down again.

'It can play tricks sometimes, make us believe things or see things that aren't exactly true.'

'But I saw him. I was there.'

Caleb clambers to his feet, graceful as cat.

'I'm talking about the other things, Maddy, about what Mr Casey told you, before . . . what they said in the basement, those stories, it was . . .'

'How do you know what they said to me –'

'They were trying to scare you, all that stuff about witches

199

and demons,' Caleb says. It's like he didn't even hear me; it's like he's reading from a script, saying lines in a play. 'That's all, just trying to keep you in line so you wouldn't run away.'

'What kind of people would do such a thing?' I ask. 'Scare somebody half to death just to make them behave?'

Caleb shakes his head. He looks at me – those massive eyes.

'It's a horrible thing to do.' I say. 'It's totally . . .'

Monstrous. That's the word in my head. But I don't say it. I bite my lip and shake my head, as the truth hits me so hard I have to back away.

They sent him here to spy on me. Anything I say, he'll tell them. Whatever's going on here, he's in on it, too.

'They want to keep you safe, Maddy,' he says. 'Seriously, that's what all of this is about. It's all about you . . .'

I feel the pulse again, so strong it almost hurts. 'What do you know about anything. What do you know about me?'

He sighs and smiles. Those white teeth. Those sparkling blue eyes with the green and gold flecks.

I think about what they said in the basement – *devil, demon* – and even before Caleb speaks I hear his words in my head.

'I know all about you, Maddy.'

I stand up, tears of horror stinging my eyes.

'No,' I say. 'No, you bloody don't.'

I grab my rucksack, but this time Caleb doesn't stop me.

'You won't be able to go anywhere, Maddy.'

He nods toward the door. There's a noise on the landing – the heavy shuffling of feet, the unmistakable rasp of Mrs Gibson's cough.

'They won't let you.'

'You want to come *home*?' Mum whines.

I'm hunched behind the headmaster's desk. I shouldn't be in this room. I shouldn't be using this phone, but what choice do I have? My own phone's been stolen, Mr Casey's is lost in that horrible basement. Afternoon assembly has just started, Mr Grayling's PA is at lunch, and I've managed to give Mrs Gibson the slip, so this is my only chance.

'Yes,' I whisper. 'As soon as I can.'

'But you're out of hospital, right?'

'Yes.'

'And they told me you were so happy to be back at Crowham.'

'They lied, Mum. They've lied about so many things. I'm not at all happy, and if you want the truth, I'm scared. It's dangerous here, Mum, I think this is a terrible place run by evil people who steal and lie and –'

'Maddy?'

'Yeah?'

'Sorry for interrupting you, darling, but . . .'

She stops talking.

'Mum?'

'. . . but if you must know, this isn't a good time for me.'

There's a silence, horrible and huge. It's like the air that circulates between us – the jet stream over the sea, the wind over the flat prairies, the powerful, invisible swoosh that swirls between the tops of mountains – all those miles, all that space.

'Maddy? Are you there? Did you hear me?'

'I heard, Mum.'

'And you've got your friends, haven't you? Can't they help you out? What was that new girl's name? The one you like so much?'

I need to answer, to get words into my mouth, but my body's gone numb and my brain has been shocked into mush.

Not a good time . . .

'Maddy?'

'Hannah,' I finally mutter. 'That's her name, but she's not here any more, Mum.'

'Oh, darling, I'm so sorry to hear that . . .'

I wait for Mum to say something else. I wait for her to tell me that she's being daft, that of course, I *must* come home, what was she thinking, that she's going online to buy a ticket right this minute and she'll straighten everything out and I'll soon be on my way back home.

But she doesn't say those things. She doesn't say anything except a quick, 'Goodbye. I love you. Hang in there, darling.'

I put the phone down, check the corridor, make sure the coast is clear.

Hang in there. Yeah, Mum, that's what I'll do.

I walk as quickly as I can without breaking into a run, and look up at the portraits that scared poor Jordan. Their stern, heartless faces don't frighten me now. Pictures can't hurt me, I have to believe that. Ghosts can't. *Fings* or men or devils can't.

Nothing can hurt me any more.

Nobody can.

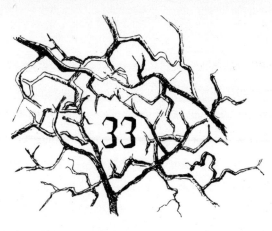

33

'Miss, Jake farted.'

The top of my plaid wool skirt scratches the bare skin underneath. It feels weird being back in lessons. Wearing the hideous winter uniform – heavy kilt, white shirt, blazer and tie. Putting up with the same stupid boys. There's a different teacher, though, and an empty desk where Hannah used to sit.

It seems wrong to be here. Disrespectful to Mr Casey whose body was taken away yesterday, only an hour after he died. I watched from my attic window after Caleb left. The ambulance arrived and drove to the back entrance. Fifteen minutes later it came around the front again, with Sir's body in a bag, stretched out on a gurney in the back.

And nobody's asked me a single question. The dinner lady knew I was with him. Missy and Mrs Gibson must have figured it out, too. It's as if they don't want to know what happened in the basement. It's like they're scared.

'Well, what do you expect me to do about it, young man?'

The supply teacher – a middle-aged woman wearing a top that's cut so low her black bra shows – writes the cover task on the board while all the boys in the class snigger.

I look over at the empty desk where Hannah used to sit. It was true, apparently, what Missy said about Hannah going back to Africa. Jordan and Darshan told me they met Hannah's aunt when she came to the school and they helped her box up Hannah's things. The woman wasn't sad or anything – it was all very jolly and she left after shaking hands with Miss Burke and Mr Grayling. And Hannah *had* gone back to Rwanda, not Cape Town, because the aunt told Darsh and Jordan about Volcanoes National Park where all the gorillas live.

So Hannah's just gone, it seems. Not kidnapped.

Maybe that voicemail wasn't really full of scary sounds or her talking about darkness or woods. Maybe the whole 'don't trust them' thing was just my own thoughts. Maybe what Caleb said was true – I've started hearing things that aren't real, including Hannah's words.

Maybe she's just moved back home, with no goodbye, and no way for me to reach her.

Open to page 223, it says on the board. *Read the text and answer the questions.* It's all about the Suffragettes – pretty tame stuff. Okay, so the women were force-fed in prison, and one of them died after throwing herself under a horse at the derby, but, hey, what's that compared with being burned at the stake or getting disembowelled in front of half the population of London?

I pretend to read what's on the page, and hunch over my exercise book so it looks like I'm writing. I listen to the sounds in the room – noses sniffing, feet shuffling, throats clearing, paper being scrunched up into balls and chucked across the room.

No screaming. No crackling flames. None of that demonic grinding or groaning.

So the interrogation I was given in the basement, the stories I was told about witches and devils – was Caleb right about that, too? Was it part of the plan to keep me from running away, just like taking my passport and debit card, letting somebody loose in my room and wrecking my stuff?

And those sounds that followed me through the darkness – they were just another manifestation of my fear, coming to life in my panic-crazed mind. What else could they have been? Really? Now that everything's back to 'normal'?

Hannah probably got it wrong about the secret library, too. We only looked at a few of the shelves. Maybe not all the books were about supernatural things. Some might have had proper writing, real stories. The library could be full of antique copies of Shakespeare or Dickens or Jane Austen.

And the other stuff?

Hannah's *badness* was just superstition. That's what Reverend Anne said, anyway – Tokoloshe was a made-up story like the Sandman or the Big Bad Wolf.

Jordan's *fings*. They could be anything, right? A little kid, abandoned by his parents, left to fend for himself in a scary old building? No wonder his imagination ran wild, like mine did. No wonder he went half-crazy with fear.

So what *is* real?

The slumped-over bodies wearing ties as tight as garrotes, collars that chafe, woollen blazers that itch and bind. They're all real.

A mother who doesn't want me and a best friend who left without saying goodbye – those things are real.

Being stuck in a place where I'm surrounded by nutters and weird hippies who dance in front of fires.

Real.

And ghosts.

A cluster of them swoosh beneath the desk, between the supply teacher's legs. I close my eyes, to clear my vision, and look again. They're still there, playing hide and seek. The pretty, silvery one pulls away from the others, does a little twirl.

I shake my head, open my textbook, doodle in the margins of my paper, but every time I look up they're still there.

Still real.

The rest of it may be lies, or tricks, or fairy stories, but the ghosts . . .

The ghosts are true.

34

Something's wrong with Natalie Ashmore.

She's still blonde, her boobs remain unfeasibly large, but she's being cheerful and chirpy again – nauseatingly sweet. What's going on?

She collars me after fourth period English. It's been three days since everything happened – since Hannah went missing, since Mr Casey died – and I've done what Sir told me to do. I've put on my school uniform and pretended those things never happened.

'Please, Maddy,' Nat purrs. 'You've got to help us.'

It's like a scene out of a stupid American TV programme. The evil cheerleader-type making friends with the nerdy girl. The nerdy girl feeling happy to be accepted by someone so popular, yet nervous – wondering if she's being set up for some humiliating payback. This is the second time she's been kind to me . . .

'Well?'

'I don't know . . .'

'We need you at Bonfire Committee more than ever now that Hannah's gone away.'

I mumble and nod vaguely. What else do I have to do? Where else can I go?

Nat smiles. 'I'll take that as a yes.'

I sit by myself on the far table where Hannah and I used to laugh and joke. Caleb's up front, perfecting his amazing float design while Natalie swans around rallying the troops. Darshan and Jordan are at the other side of the room, their little heads together as they lean into the centre of the table, totally absorbed in their task. I think back to their first day – Darshan's tears, Jordan's *fings* – and it seems so long ago.

I'm cutting out more paper flames – we need yellow apparently – when Natalie shouts for everyone's attention and Miss Burke swans into the room. She stands beside Nat, looking business-like and sombre. Her hair is pulled back and twisted into a bun. She's wearing black wide-legged trousers and a grey cardigan. Sad and serious clothes.

'I want to thank you all for being here today,' Missy says. 'I know how hard it is for all of us. Mr Casey was a . . .'

She has to stop. Compose herself.

'He was a marvellous teacher and a valued colleague, but we owe it to him to make the Crowham Martyrs School float part of the best Bonfire Night parade in history.'

Caleb and Nat stand up. Everybody applauds – but the whole spectacle makes me feel sick. What do these people know about how Sir died? They weren't there. I still see it so clearly. The look on his face, the crazy things he muttered, the way the breath left his body as if something had him by the throat, as if some horrible *fing* –

The smell of patchouli brings me back to reality. When I open my eyes Missy's sitting on the chair opposite me, cutting into a piece of green card with a pair of scissors, keeping her eyes on her work.

'Glad to see you're back in the swing of things, Maddy.'

I've managed to avoid her since what happened in the basement – I've stayed in my room most of the time – but she and Mrs Gibson keep tabs on me, and not very subtly either. Missy's perfume lingers in the corridors between my lessons, Mrs Gibson's footsteps are on regular attic stairs patrol, and every night, one of them sits in front of the fire in the entrance hall, watching the door. What do they think is going to happen? I'm going to sneak out under cover of darkness? How can I with no money or passport, with nobody who's willing to take me in?

'There's no point in worrying about what never happened, is there? To Hannah, I mean.'

Missy puts down the scissors, leans over with her hands held out as if she wants me to take them.

'And besides, you know you can't leave.'

I push my chair away from the table.

'Your mother wants you here, Maddy. She already told you, didn't she?'

I swallow hard, trying to stay calm. How does she know I called Mum? Did she follow me into the office? Listen to the conversation?

Or was it the other way around? Did Mum tell Missy to stop me from calling, so she can get on with her wonderful, daughter-free life over in sunny California?

Missy sighs indulgently, and looks out one of the tall windows as a car pulls in from the main road and crunches up the driveway. 'We've got a visitor,' she says. 'It's Hannah's aunt, Patience. Perhaps you'd like to meet her.'

The wind outside is blowing a gale – battering the trees, tearing leaves away from branches and twisting them around in swirly dust clouds. I watch the car stop outside the doorway and see the driver get out. She walks up to the door with a brisk stride. She's tall and pretty – just like Hannah's mum.

I wait a few minutes before following Missy to the entrance hall. I listen through the open doorway, still not sure if I should go in or not. What good would it do me to talk to her? What if Hannah's never even mentioned me? How would I feel then?

Missy and Hannah's aunt stand in front of the fire, whispering. When I go through the doorway, they stop and turn around. The visitor smiles. Her teeth are as perfect as Hannah's mum's, her dimples are as soft.

'You must be Maddy,' she says, rushing across the floor to take me in her arms and give me a massive hug. 'Hannah has told me much about you.'

'She has?' I can't help but smile.

'Of course,' the woman says. Her African accent is a stronger version of Hannah's. 'You are like family to us now.'

Missy butts in. 'I'm sorry, Maddy – let me introduce you to Patience Masupha.'

The woman smiles again and takes my hand. Then her look becomes more serious. 'We are so sorry about upsetting you and giving you such a fright,' she says. 'But Hannah was needed at home and she's now with her family.'

Missy is still next to the fire, smiling smugly. 'I'm sure Hannah will be in touch as soon as everything settles down,' she says. 'Isn't that right, Miss Masupha?'

'Of course, Miss Burke.'

There are more handshakes, another lung-clearing hug, and then Hannah's aunt says goodbye.

A gust of wind catches the door as she leaves, flinging it wide open and banging it shut. The chandelier sways in the draft. The fireplace embers spark and glow.

'I'm glad Hannah's okay,' I say grudgingly.

Missy latches the door.

'There was never any need to worry, Maddy.'

Her body twitches suddenly, as if she's caught a chill. She steps over to the wicker basket beside the fireplace, picks up a log and places it carefully in the middle of the fire.

'Hannah has always been safe.'

A few minutes later and I'm hunkering behind the desk in the records office. I listen – no heavy footsteps – and take a deep breath. No perfume.

My heart beats with excitement – is it the thrill of breaking the rules? Of knowing I'm not allowed to be in this room, and not supposed to be making this call? Or is it just the thought of being able to talk to Hannah, to tell her everything that's going on?

I take out her student folder, ready to punch in the number.

There's Hannah's picture, with her birthday on the back. There's the name of the school in Cape Town, her parents' names, and the address and number for them in Rwanda.

I punch in the phone number and wait. The line has a slight hiss, like when I call Mum in LA. The ring is like an English one, though – *bring bring, bring bring.* As soon as I hear it, my heart starts to pound, and I'm already smiling, anticipating the sound of Hannah's voice.

'Hello?'

That's not Hannah – it must be her mum.

'Hi, is this Mrs Masupha-Harris?

'Yes.'

'I'm calling for Hannah.'

A pause.

'Who is this?'

'I'm calling from England.'

'Is this the school?' The voice on the phone sounds strained, anxious.

'Yes,' I say.

'Is that you, Anne?'

Anne. She must mean Reverend Anne.

'Yes,' I lie.

'Are you calling about Hannah?'

'Yes.'

There's another, longer pause. I hear shuffling sounds, a muffled whisper. My heart's beating faster than ever, but it's not with excitement any more.

'Is everything all right over there, Anne?'

I don't answer. Obviously, it isn't. Hannah's *not* with her parents like they told me; she's not at home.

'What is going on?' Hannah's mother asks. 'Has something happened to my daughter?'

What can I say? Why did I call? My hands are shaking and I want to blurt out the truth, but I'm too frightened to speak.

'Hello? Hello?'

I can hear the fear in her voice, but I still say nothing.

'You told us they'd look after her at that school,' Hannah's mum says. 'You promised us she would be safe . . .'

When I creep back into the entrance hall, Missy's still at the fire, standing close to the flames. She's swaying, like before, but this time I can hear music, too. It's high-pitched and whiny – is Missy singing to herself?

No, you couldn't call it singing. It's more like a chant. A weird sort of prayer. What's the word? An incantation.

Outside the stained-glass window, the wind howls and rages. Somewhere in the distance – Crowham village most likely – fireworks and rockets pop and bang in the run-up to tomorrow night's big Bonfire Night display.

Another huge blast of wind bashes the building, rattling the stained glass. I look up at the window, and for the first time I recognise who's in the picture – it's St Michael, Archangel and Protector, from the church. He's holding up his sword ready to swoop down on the snakes and demon-like lizards that writhe and hiss beneath his feet. They look alive in the firelight, and the sound of hissing flames seems to come from their mouths.

The wind intensifies. Missy's voice gets louder and the flames in the fireplace leap higher, burn brighter.

With her hands held high, Missy edges even nearer, and the heat fans her wide trousers, twisting them around her legs.

'Missy!' I shout. 'Be careful!'

She lowers her hands. The wind gets quieter, even the flames die down.

She turns around, looks at me blankly.

'The fire,' I say.

She shakes her head, as if waking herself.

'Yes, Madeline? What about the fire?'

She turns away again, brushing bits of soot off her jacket, smoothing her trousers. She picks up a broom that's leaning against the hearth. She sweeps the ashes off the floor, all the while muttering that strange, witchy chant.

It's not as scary the second time around.

The hidden corridor leading to the library is just as narrow, the carpet's blood-coloured stains are still visible. My heart skips a beat as the pipes clank and rumble, but other than that, I'm totally calm.

The entire school is at the Bonfire Parade in Crowham village – except me, that is, and the Catholic kids who aren't keen on the idea of watching the pope being burned in effigy along with the prime minster and this year's Bonfire villain – so the building is as empty and silent as a tomb.

I thought Missy would force me to go with all the others – give me some sickening pep talk about Team Crowham or, even worse, needing to honour all the work Mr Casey put into the making the float – but she seemed happy when I said I didn't want to go.

Relieved, almost.

She left Mrs Gibson behind to keep watch. She's squeezed

into a padded armchair smack in the middle of the entrance hall, so she's not likely to check up on me. When I looked over the mezzanine railing she was scowling at the barred and bolted door as if she was expecting intruders, and daring them to break in.

I turn the handle to the library door. Silently – no creaking or groaning – the door opens. I take my pen light out of my dressing-gown pocket, click it on.

In the dim, wavering glow, the room looks just like it did when I was here with Hannah. I circle the huge central table – books are stacked in the same precarious towers, and the ones we took have been put back in the right places. What exactly am I looking for?

Evidence. Clues. Answers.

Missy lied about Hannah – that wasn't her aunt and she didn't go home to her parents. So where is she? And why did they lie?

And what about Missy's strange behaviour in front of the fire – those weird incantations? Could what Mr Casey said be true? Could there really be witches and demons here at Crowham? Are the *badness* and *fings* real? And do all these things have anything to do with Hannah going missing? Do they have anything to do with *me*?

I shine my light on the floor.

Footprints. Totally human this time. Although they've been smudged, it's easy to follow the trail – behind a row of bookcases, back to the centre of the room, and across the floor to another group of shelves. What was this person looking for? A specific book? A secret passageway?

The footprints stop in front of one of the bookcases. All the volumes are packed in tightly, with no obvious gaps. I shine my light on the spines. Those weird symbols again, a title that could be in Latin – *Malefecus* something or other. I look for other books, proper ones like *Pride and Prejudice* or *Oliver Twist,* but all the spines show symbols that seem more ancient than any language – swirls and triangular shapes.

The only book in English is on the top shelf – *The Lore of Demons.* I stand on tiptoes and hold up my light. It's not just the English that makes this book different. It's been pulled out slightly, so that it juts out in front of the other books. It isn't caked with dust like all the other books either. Someone has taken *The Lore of Demons* down and given it a clean.

I reach for the book, taking it slowly off the shelf, half-expecting an alarm to sound or a secret wall panel to open. Nothing happens – no earthquake, no thunder.

I run my fingers across the book's smooth, soft cover. The leather looks burnished and shiny, as if it's been oiled, and the gold letters sparkle in the light.

I rearrange the shelf so that it's impossible to see where a book's been taken. I wipe my feet on the floor, erasing my prints, and the ones of the person who led me here. It's not a very convincing covering of tracks, but it's good enough, I hope. Good enough to buy some time, good enough to keep the others – whoever they are – at bay for a while.

Back in my room, I run my hands along the book's front cover, stroke the spine, the back, the gold-burnished edges of the paper. *Open it, Maddy.* I can almost hear Hannah, having a go at me for being scared. *It's just a book, Mads – words can't hurt you, can they?*

I think of what people have said about me – those words *can* hurt. *I know who you are, Maddy.* That's what Mr Casey said after I was sick behind the stage. I ignored it at the time, laughed off everything he said, thought it was all a lie or a trick. But now I wonder.

The Lore of Demons. What exactly was Mr Casey trying to tell me – what could devils or demons have to do with me?

I run my hands along the smooth surface of the book one last time before opening it. On the inside, the title pages are thin, delicate, translucent. There's an engraved picture of a *fleur de lys*, exactly like the one on the Crowham Martyrs insignia, and tiny print at the bottom says that it was published by Cloak and Ferry publishers, London, in 1798.

I lick the tip of my middle finger and turn to the first page, but it isn't there. Neither is the second page, or the third …

Hundreds of pages have been cut away, leaving nothing but the edges, and a hollowed out space – a secret, makeshift box.

So *The Lore of Demons* is just a hiding place. And inside it? Five small envelopes, yellowing with age – stamped letters, postmarked Crowham, Sussex, all addressed to the same person. Miss Mary Deeprose, 14 Almsworth Gardens, London SW12.

Mary Deeprose – is she related to us? She must be, otherwise why would she have the same name? It's not a common name, really.

I take out the first letter. 12 December, 1999.

Dear Mary,

We need you to come home. You don't know what you're getting into. Please, you need to be where it's safe – away from him.

Love, L

The second is dated 22 January, 2000.

Dear Mary,

Just back from London. They told me you've moved house, but I don't believe them. I beg you, my darling. Listen to us. You must come home, where you will be safe. It's the only way we can protect you

Love, A

The third date is months later, but the letter's been sent to the same address.

Dear Mary,

You know who he is, don't you? Why he is with you? Do you think he loves you? You're wrong. What he feels for you is the opposite of love. Please, please, listen to us!

Your adoring A

The fourth is dated May, 2001.

Dear Mary,

It's not too late. Please! Come back! There's no other way, no other place for you now. You must get away from him.

Love, A

The final letter has no date, but I recognise the handwriting. I know who it's from.

Darling Mary,

We know what you have done, the danger you are both in. Please, please come back to Crowham. If not for your own safety, then for your child's. We can protect you here. It's the only place. The only way.

Your loving Susie

Susie. Susannah. Mum.

Why would my mother be writing a letter to someone I've never heard of, asking her to come back home? Why would she be warning of danger, and why would that letter be stashed in a book about demons? Hidden in a secret library where I've been sent to school – where *she* sent me?

I read the letters again. *Mary.* Mum must have some relatives I don't know about. Long lost cousins? This Mary must have got into some kind of trouble – a boyfriend the family didn't approve of or something. But why have I never heard of her?

I take off my dressing gown, slip under the covers. I put the letters back into their envelopes and set them carefully back into the little casket, one on top of each other. I get to the last letter, the one written by Susie – Mum, that is. I turn it over, fold it –

There's more on the other side, still in Mum's writing.

We were the last, Mary. We should have remained the last. When our kind dies out, his kind dies, too.
Now, because of your baby, it continues.

My darling Mary, what have you done?

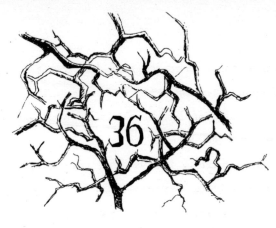

36

Rough sea, rocky coastline, narrow strip of sand.

A rising tide. The waves getting closer, crashing hard at our feet.

Mum holding me tightly, arms around my waist, pulling me backwards, hoisting me up, up, up to the top.

Safe. Flat ground, stony and sandy. Tufty grass, prickly thick-leaved plants with faded pink flowers.

Mum laughing, her bright smile. 'See, Maddy? Told you not to be scared.'

We stand up, brush ourselves off, look down for a moment at the cauldron of foam against rock. Mum takes my hand and we head back towards the land, towards the solid ground, back towards –

Something. Standing in our way.

Dark, like a shadow.

Some*one*. A man.

I'm woken by a knock at the door.

Instantly, I remember the strange letters in the hollowed out book. I check under my pillow.

The book is still there. Safe.

And the dream. I close my eyes – what was it?

A man. Not just his hand this time, his whole body, his face.

I close my eyes, trying to remember what he looked like, not sure if I'm awake or still asleep and dreaming.

Another knock.

I pull the covers up to my neck, keep my eyes on the door.

The next knock is louder, and I hear a child's voice call out my name. 'Maddy? Are you there?'

It must be Jordan. I slip out of bed, rush to the door. I can ask him about the *fings*, find out exactly what it is he sees. If I show him the pictures in the book, maybe he'll recognise something.

I open the door, and Darshan stumbles in. His teeth chatter and he's shivering, even though he's wearing his pyjamas and a heavy dressing gown. 'Jordan's not in his bed,' he whispers.

His brown eyes are wet with tears. 'We went to sleep after we got back from the village, but when I woke up a bit later he wasn't in the room. I checked the corridors, up and down, but . . .'

I close the door. 'Have you checked the toilets?'

He nods, lets out a cry. 'What if the scary man has come –'

'Did you check the loos, Darsh?'

He nods.

'What about the refectory?'

He shudders, shakes his head. 'I don't like that place. I never go there on my own, not without . . .' He lets out another sob. 'Not without Jordan.'

'Don't worry, Darsh, we'll find him.'

I throw a sweatshirt over my pyjamas, pull on warm, woolly socks and slip into a pair of old trainers. I take the pen light from my desk drawer. The battery probably won't last long, but it's better than nothing.

Darshan follows me down the attic stairs and we creep along the girls' corridor. I look into the bathroom for good measure – who knows, Jordan might have used it if he was afraid of what he imagined was lurking in the boys'.

There's no one – just the empty toilet stalls, the shower cubicles, a leaky tap in one of the sinks. Back outside, we pass the bedrooms, creep towards the main corridor, stopping at the back staircase the cleaners use.

'This way,' I whisper.

Darshan shakes his head.

'Come on. There's no time.'

'It's forbidden.'

'What is?'

'That staircase is not for student use. It says so in the student guide. It is only for the use of –'

I open the door, pull him through.

'But the guide said . . .'

I bend down and look into his dark, moist eyes. 'Darshan . . . if we are going to find Jordan we might have to break some rules. Do you understand that?'

He nods half-heartedly. Sniffs.

'You may have to go rogue, Darsh.'

He nods a little more vigorously and his eyes light up.

'Rogue?'

He smiles at me, excited now.

'Rogue.'

The refectory is empty. There's a noise from the kitchen that makes Darshan jump and gasp, but it's just the fridge freezer motor, kicking into life. If Jordan had been here, it would have been to make a snack – toast or crumpets, a mug of hot chocolate – but there are no crumbs on the worktops, no sloshes of milk or cocoa on the floor.

'Maddy?'

When I turn around Darshan's standing at the door to the basement. 'What is in *here*?'

'Nothing,' I say. 'Stand away from the door.'

He doesn't move. He jiggles the handle a few times.

'No, Darshan. I told you not to touch it –'

He touches the key, smiles. 'But I am going rogue.'

I stagger towards him, trying to reach his hand before he can unlock the door, but blood rushes to my head, my vision blurs, and the room spins as I wobble and sway. 'Please, Darshan, don't –'

Somehow I manage to lower myself to the floor before I fall. Darshan rushes to my side. 'Sorry, Maddy, I won't go rogue again. I promise.' He puts his arm on my shoulder. 'Not without your permission.'

It only takes a few seconds for my head to clear. I get up carefully and look at the basement door. It all comes back to me – the interrogation room, the boxes, Mr Casey's final minutes of life, the horrible sounds, the ghosts, the –

Footsteps.

Darshan clutches my hand, his eyes wide.

'Someone's coming, Maddy.'

I look around the room for hiding places. The cupboard under the worktop – too full of pots and pans. I try another. Tinned food, crammed tight in neat stacks and rows.

The footsteps get louder. A shadow passes the window in the kitchen door.

'Maddy,' Darshan whispers.

He's standing at the basement door again; key in hand, ready to unlock it.

I nod. My stomach's already twisting with fear – whatever was down there before could be waiting for us – but whatever's coming to find us now could be worse – and it's really here.

Darshan opens the door, and I join him at the threshold. I step on to the staircase first, holding his hand, leading him down into the darkness. There's no ghostly barricade to help us this time, just a few skinny waifs that shiver like strands of old Christmas tinsel.

'Wait here,' I say, as I clamber back up the stairs.

There are sounds from the kitchen. Muffled footsteps – man or woman, it's impossible to tell, but they're just on the other side of the door. I put my ear against it, listening for breath or the shuffling of feet.

Below me, Darshan whimpers. I put my hand up and shush him, but I doubt if he can hear me. The thin blanket of ghost hovers near him, thickening.

The footsteps move away, get fainter.

I open the door a crack. Whoever is in the kitchen is standing on the opposite side of the room. Below me,

Darshan shifts and fidgets. I put my hand up again, hoping he'll stay still and quiet for a few more seconds, until I can see who –

Dark hair. Broad shoulders. A solid outline even in this dim light.

Caleb.

'Maddy?' he whispers.

I close the door. Lock it.

'If you're looking for Jordan,' Caleb says, 'I know where to find him.'

How would he know? How *could* he?

'Hannah, too – I know where she is.'

He's waiting for me to say something. Does he think I'm so weak or stupid that I'll give myself away?

'You've got to come out of there, Maddy.'

Darshan crawls up the stairs on his hands and knees. He sits one step below me, huddling at my feet.

'You must know that you're in terrible danger.'

Darshan pulls at my leg. He looks up at me, his eyes wide with terror. I put my left hand out and cover his mouth to prevent him from screaming.

'You're *all* in danger, Maddy, but if you come out of there, if you get back to somewhere safer . . .'

I hold my breath. Darshan clings to my leg.

233

From the other side of the door I feel the pulse, and before Caleb speaks, I hear his words in my head –

'Maybe it won't be too late.'

How did he do that?

Suddenly, it's as if I can see him through the door. Those bright eyes, so strange and so familiar, and I remember that connection I felt the night he arrived. *Too late for what?* I want to ask, but I know I can't trust him. It's a trick, nothing more.

'Did you hear me, Maddy?'

The handle shakes and rattles and heavy fists bash the wood.

'Come on, Maddy.'

Caleb's pushing his body against the door, desperate to break it down.

'I'll tell you everything if you just let me in.'

No, I think, hurrying down the stairs, taking Darshan's hand. *Don't listen, Maddy.*

'The whole truth, Maddy,' Caleb shouts. 'I mean it this time.'

The light from my torch flickers and fades.

I drag Darshan behind me, but this time he doesn't resist. There's another staircase here somewhere, the one Missy, Mr Casey and Mrs Gibbons bundled me down – but where is it?

'Hurry, Darsh,' I whisper.

Behind us there's a massive thud – is that Caleb? Has he smashed the door down? Can he be that strong?

Footsteps – too heavy to be Caleb's – thump behind us in the darkness.

Darshan stumbles and I pull him back up. Dust fills my lungs again. Strands of yuck – dead bugs caught up in spider webs – flit across my face, stick to my hair.

As we hurtle through the darkness, I'm no longer aware of the footsteps. I hear nothing but my own breathing and the scuffling of Darshan's feet on the dirty floor. We mustn't stop. We mustn't slow down or look back.

The words that Mrs Gibson and Mr Casey used ring in my ears.

Devil. Demon.

Faster and faster, we duck and weave through bits of tattered cloth that hang like curtains, and we manage to avoid the trunks and boxes set out like obstacles to slow us down. I cast my eyes into the shadows – if only there was a place to hide, to rest for a moment.

There's light ahead. Faint, but visible. Maybe it's the window well where I tried to build the pyramid. Maybe those are the lights from above ground, seeping into the basement. That would mean we're close to the main entrance, near the other staircase. This is the way out, I think – the way to safety!

Darshan lets out a scream. He lets go of my hand and tumbles to the ground, landing with a massive thud.

'Darsh?'

I stay still, listening. I can't hear anything except Darshan's whimpering – no footsteps behind us, no breathing, no movement.

'I think I hurt myself, Maddy. I . . . I can't move.'

I bend over, not daring to touch him.

'Where does it hurt, Darsh?'

'My arm. I think it's –'

The pen light has just enough juice left to let me see that his wrist has been twisted backwards and is already swelling.

'Looks like a bad sprain at least,' I whisper, 'so try not to move your hand, okay?'

He bites his lip, sniffs a few times, nodding bravely.

I hold him by the shoulders and help him back on to his feet. We stand still for a moment, and as we both strain to listen, something rumbles behind us – a deep throaty growl.

Devil. Demon. That's not Caleb's voice – it can't be. Is it what was here before?

Darshan's body trembles, and his legs are wobbling. I tighten my grip on his shoulders – if we don't move quickly he'll collapse with the terror, but which way should we go?

Behind us, there's another growl, and I remember the footprints beside Mr Casey's body – the massive claws.

And in front of us?

The ghosts are back, flickering in a dark, distant corner – a dull beacon.

'This way, Darsh.' He hesitates for a second, and stumbles forward.

'Follow the light.'

In this part of the basement the path isn't clear. There are bits of wood, piles of rubble in our way. The ghosts are getting brighter, though, making it easier for me to see. I squeeze Darshan's shoulder, draw him closer.

'Nearly there,' I say.

'Where?'

'Somewhere safer, I think.'

As we approach the light, I slow down. The strange glow hovers like a dim planet.

'But how do you know, Maddy?'

'I'm following the light.'

'What light?'

'It's there, Darsh. Believe me.'

Behind us, the footsteps get closer. In front of us, the light glows brighter as one ghost breaks away from the cluster – it's the silvery, shimmery one.

'Let's go,' I whisper.

The shiny ghost moves away again, leading us into the depths of the basement. Out of reach, I hope. Somewhere safe.

Darshan stumbles as we move forward.

'I can't see anything, Maddy.'

'Don't worry, Darsh. I can.'

The ghost swirls and flickers, guiding us deeper and deeper into the dark.

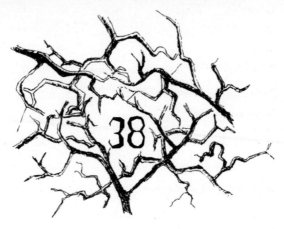

38

No more footsteps or strange noises. No more whoever or whatever that was. No more anything, for now at least.

'I'm tired, Maddy,' Darshan whispers. 'Can we stop for a minute?'

'Okay,' I say. 'It should be safe enough here.'

We sit on the floor, lean against something solid – a wall? A door? It takes a while for my eyes to adjust, but we seem to be in a cupboard or a narrow corridor used for storage. Old doors are suspended from the ceiling on chains. Furniture is stacked up against the wall – wooden tables with ornately carved legs, heavy chests of drawers with delicate inlaid veneers.

Darshan rests against my shoulder, his whole body quivering. Poor kid. He doesn't see ghosts or *fings* or scary men, so he's not used to this kind of terror. He's in excruciating pain and wandering about in total darkness with no way of knowing why he's stuck here or what this might be about.

And what *is* this about? *I know who you are*, Mr Casey said. *Our kind*, Mum wrote in a letter to some relative I've never heard of. Is this all about the ghosts? Mr Casey said as much when I was in that interrogation room. They all knew, he said – he and Missy and Mrs Gibson. Maybe Mum can see ghosts, too, and maybe she told everyone at Crowham what freaks we are.

But what kind of freaks *are* we? And why have my friends gone missing? Is that about the ghosts, too? *Maybe it won't be too late*, Caleb said. *What won't be too late?* I close my eyes for a moment, even though I'm already in darkness. There are so many things I don't understand. My head throbs and spins with pictures – the man in my dreams, Missy's strange incantation in front of the fire, the etchings of witches and devils. I remember the sounds, too – the screaming of tortured women, the clinking chains and creaking ropes, the spitting, raging fires. The Crowham Martyrs – is that who I'm hearing?

Beside me, Darshan stirs. 'Maddy?'

'Yeah, Darsh?'

'Listen.'

I strain to pick a sound out of the silence, and for a few seconds I wonder if Darshan's imagining things, too, teetering on the edge of insanity like me.

'It's here again,' Darshan whispers.

A deep groan comes from an invisible corner of the basement.

A growling.

Darshan nestles in closer. My heart picks up speed, fluttering wildly – if both of us can hear it, then it must be real. It's almost like the other noises – the crackling fire and screams I heard before I collapsed, or the horrible grinding that chased me through the basement after Mr Casey died.

But it's not the same.

It's a *voice* – pitched so low I can feel vibrations in my chest.

'Is that Caleb, Maddy?'

'I don't think so.'

But who can it be? The dark man? The scary man? The *one more monstrous?*

I hold my breath, clutching Darshan's trembling body, shielding him as best I can. I must be brave, I think. I must be brave for him.

'Is it getting closer, Maddy?'

There's a shuffling sound, like feet on the floor, only softer, padded – like massive claws. I hear breathing – a raspy snarl. It isn't getting louder, though. Wherever it is, *whatever* it is, it seems as lost as we are.

'Maddy?'

'Shhh.'

It's totally dark again; the dim globe has disappeared. Have even the ghosts abandoned us?

We wait. Keep still.

The padded footsteps move in circles – closer to us, away. The husky growl gets louder, then fainter, then louder, then fainter. After a while I realise what's happening – whatever is out there is taunting us, playing with us like a cat stalking a mouse.

'Are you sure that's not Caleb?'

'I'm sure, Darsh.'

The footsteps stop – some distance away. But the growling carries on – a gravelly one-note burr that slowly changes. It sounds like babbling, or some language I've never heard before, and I'm picturing an animal – a wolf or a lion, standing on two legs and trying to talk.

Darshan nestles still closer, whimpering softly. I put one hand softly over his mouth – he has to be quiet – and cradle his head against my shoulder with the other.

The sound goes back to the growly hum. I hear footsteps again, loping away, getting fainter and fainter until at last there's no sound at all – no strange words, no growl, no dragging feet.

'Maddy?'

'Quiet, Darsh. Please.'

'Do you ever see strange things, like what Jordan sees?'

Mum's warning rings in my ears. Never tell. Remember what happened to Hannah. To Mr Casey.

'No,' I whisper. 'I only see what's real.'

We sit for a few more minutes, taking in the silence, trembling with cold and fear.

'I can hear things,' Darshan says. He sniffs, lifts his good arm to wipe his nose on the back of his dressing gown sleeve. 'Like that doggy man who was just here.'

Darshan's bony shoulders shiver against mine. He's cold now, as well as terrified. I wish I had something for him to put on, something warm and comforting.

'Jordan can see things,' he says, 'but I only hear.'

'Did he ever tell you what those things looked like?' I ask.

'Of course,' Darshan says. 'But they weren't always the same.'

'No?'

'Sometimes they were like movie monsters. Big and hairy with ginormous claws and teeth. Sometimes they were people – dead ones that walk funny. What are they called?'

'Zombies,' I say.

Darshan's body shudders again. 'But the worst ones,' he sniffs, 'have horns.'

'Like animals, you mean – rhinos? Bulls?'

Darshan shakes his head, leans closer to me.

'Not like animals,' he whispers. 'Like the scary man. Like the man in the toilet who had horns.'

Darshan snores gently. He's been out for about fifteen minutes, and it feels quiet and settled here. I'll let him sleep. When he wakes up we can find a staircase – a way out – and start hunting properly for Hannah and Jordan.

I listen for the sounds of growling, for footsteps or breathing, even for the familiar sound of Caleb's normal, human voice. I keep my eyes open, in case I can catch a glimpse of whatever was out there – zombie, devil, monster, *fing*.

I yawn. So hard to hold back the exhaustion. So tired and empty from running in the dark. Must keep my eyes open. Must not sleep . . .

A bed. Soft, with a fluffy pillow and crisp white sheets. An open window. Fresh air. I'm dreaming – I have to be.

The sea. Gulls soaring overhead.

Mum.

Smiling.

Blue sky. Blonde hair. The vast ocean. The wind.

'Run, Maddy.'

A darkening cloud, dulling the sky – lead-grey, heavy.

'Now, Maddy. Run away.'

The cloud closing in, getting blacker, bigger, so close to us that Mum has to step backwards towards the cliff – only it's not a cloud, it's a man.

The man.

'Mummy, stop!'

'There's no other way, Maddy.'

I don't move. I can't. It's a dream and I'm stuck, as if my feet are glued to the ground, and I can't run away, I can't do anything, I can only open my eyes, open my eyes and –

'Mummy! You're going to fall.'

She looks at me, shining eyes full of love, not fear, and I see her for what she is – not my mum, not Susannah Deeprose, but some other woman, more beautiful than Susannah, more beautiful than anyone –

'Go, Maddy!' As the man presses in on her, she steps backwards, towards the edge of the cliff, towards the jagged rocks below, towards the swirling sea.

'This is your only chance, darling – you must run away.'

She takes another step. She's –

I open my eyes.

Remember, Maddy.

It's there. Right in front of me. What I witnessed all those years ago.

I watch the woman – my mum, my *real* mother – step off the cliff. I see the bit of scruffy gorse that catches on her foot as she stumbles backwards.

I hear the scream, cut off a few seconds later by a brutal thud.

I see the cloud that isn't a cloud, watch it hover over the solid ground and swoop down towards the sea, like a terrible, monstrous bird.

I don't follow it, though. I back away.

I don't go to the edge to see if my mother is still alive, if she can be saved.

I run.

I run and run and run.

I never stop.

In the real world, the dark has grown a shadow. Someone stands over us, looking down.

'My mother's name isn't Susannah, is it?' I say to the darkness, to whatever or whoever it is, because I'm sure it knows.

'No.' It's a woman's voice. Not unkind. Not cruel.

I smell the patchouli. Missy. She steps closer, and I can see her, too.

'My mother's dead.'

No answer. Just a nod.

'Her name was Mary,' I say. 'I found the letters.'

Beside me, Darshan moans in his half-sleep, but right now I don't care about his pain or his fear. I don't care about finding Jordan. I don't even care about Hannah.

I didn't help my own mother so why I should be bothered to help my friends?

'Oh, Maddy,' Missy sniffs. 'I loved your mum so much. We all did.'

Loved. Missy's known along.

'I saw it happen,' I whisper. 'I was there, on that clifftop, I remember.'

It's weird, but I can smell my real mother. *Her* perfume – fresh and green like the sea, tangy and flowery. I see her face clearly for the first time – blonde curls, sparkling eyes like glittery sapphires. Not the woman who calls herself my mum. Not the actress, the imposter.

Shuffling footsteps in the darkness, that wheezy growl – the monster is back. Missy looks into the darkness. She hears it, she *knows.*

'You've got to come with me,' Missy whispers.

Darshan's awake again, his breath shallow.

Memories flash into my mind, like photographs. Random,

happy things – warm beach sand between my toes, a doll in a wonky pram, a green-frosted birthday cake with my name in pink and blue icing.

'You knew she was dead?'

'Maddy, please.'

'All this time and you never said a word?'

Missy leans over Darshan, lifts him by the waist and holds him awkwardly,

'It's time to go. Time to get away before ...'

Missy peers into the darkness.

'What you saw remember was real, Maddy, and the ... the ...'

Why is Missy struggling to find the words? Is the truth so hard for her to tell?

'The ... *man* who caused your mother's death –'

Missy sputters and wheezes as the footsteps get louder. The animal voice – rough and treacly, deeper than any I've ever heard – growls in anger and frustration.

Missy chokes out the words. 'He is coming for you.'

The ghost is waiting in my room. She twirls in the fireplace, like a slender wisp of smoke.

Missy told me to lock the door, let no one in, stay put.

Don't make a sound, she said. *No shouting, whatever happens – don't draw attention to yourself.*

There was no time to explain, she'd said, and when I asked for the truth about where Hannah and Jordan were, she rushed away – to deal with Darshan's wrist, she'd said.

'But you must not leave this attic,' she whispered from the doorway. 'It's the safest place in the school. *We've made it safe.*'

I go to the window, but a flash of lightning and a crash of thunder shakes the glass, and I'm jolted back into the centre of the room – that was so close, the light was so blinding, the thunder so fierce.

He is coming for you.

No. That can't be true. Whatever was in the basement

couldn't have been a man. Not the man I remember, the man I saw on that clifftop all those years ago. He was a human being, at least, he didn't snarl like a –

My mother is dead.

The words in my head feel like punches. Sharp body blows.

My. Mother. Is. Dead.

I slump down on to the bed, struggling to breathe.

Somebody killed her. *Boom.*

I was there. *Pow.*

Nothing else matters – the devil books, the secret library, the stupid ghosts, that monster or whatever it is that's roaming around in the basement, ready to what – gobble me up?

My real mum is dead. Missy knew. Susannah – the one who claimed to be my mother – knew.

A floorboard on my staircase creaks. There's a knock on the door. Tap, tap, tap.

He is coming for you.

Another tap, the shuffling of feet, a raspy cough.

'Maddy?'

It's not a man, or a monster – it's Mrs Gibson, a nasty old cook.

'Maaa-deee.' She tries out a high sing-song voice, trying to sound kind and jolly. I can almost see the carving knife in her hand, polished and glistening, the point as sharp as a razor, ready to cut out my heart, roast it for Sunday lunch.

'Miss Burke asked me to check up on you, Maddy. Could you open the door?'

I think of the interrogation room, the anger on Mrs Gibson's scowling face, the way she banged the table. Even if she doesn't have a knife, she could rip my heart out with those beefy fists.

'Oh, come on, Maddy. They've all abandoned you in your hour of need – Miss Burke, those irritating friends of yours, Mr Casey . . .'

She chuckles. 'Course Sir's dead, so we can't really blame him, can we?'

A silence. I flinch – here comes another punch.

'Just like your mother.'

Anger rises up in me, churns like lava, and I bite my lip to keep from shouting out.

'Dead, I mean.'

Don't listen, Maddy.

'Do you remember her, Maddy? Your real mother?'

I shake my head, trying to dislodge her words.

'Lovely, she was. Weak, but lovely.'

Mrs Gibson rattles the door handle.

'Shame she had to die so young, but that's what happens when you disobey the rules. It's not like she wasn't warned.'

She tries the door again, gives it a little push, but it's still not enough.

'Always sad when the young ones go, isn't it, Maddy? The pretty ones?'

A gust of wind bashes a branch against my window pane.

'Like that Hannah. Such a lovely girl.'

I gasp, and clap my hand over my mouth to stop shouting out. Why is Mrs Gibson talking about Hannah?

'Or the little blond boy. What's his name?'

Jordan. I almost say it, but stop myself in time. Does she know where he is?

Of course she doesn't. The horrid old bat is just trying it on. She doesn't know a thing about either Jordan or Hannah. She's probably not even sure if I'm here. She'll give up in a minute if I can manage to keep my mouth shut.

Boom! She takes another crack at the door. Another massive thud.

I back into the bathroom and close the door. There's my rucksack, still waiting for me, all packed, ready to go.

Mrs Gibson grunts and groans on the landing. One final push and the door swings open, bashing against the wall.

I peek through the keyhole. She's looking around the room, the skin of her neck rolling in waves as she walks, like the ruffling feathers of some overstuffed bird.

She goes to the fireplace, picks up the iron poker and brandishes it like a sword, slicing the air so it makes a noisy swoosh. What's she doing – taking practice shots? Working out the perfect speed and angle to knock me over in a single blow?

She turns. Swings again. Takes a step forward, tries another swing, using both hands this time.

She loses her balance, crashing on to my bed as the poker clatters to the floor.

I rush into the room before she manages to right herself. I grab the poker, wave it wildly about. I think of St Michael, Archangel and Protector – the way he looks in the stained-glass windows, soaring through the air, bright eyes blazing, ready to take anyone on.

Beside me, the silvery ghost has twisted herself tightly, like a wound spring ready to uncoil – is she ready to take Mrs Gibson on, too?

Mrs Gibson stands up, adjusts her tabard.

'You always seemed so special, didn't you?' she hisses. 'So superior to me.'

I take a swing at her, forcing her towards the door. I feel that strange surge of energy running through my veins, strengthening my grip on the poker.

'But where is your power now, traitor?'

What is she talking about? *Power? Traitor?* Who have I betrayed?

'You know he'll get her,' she croaks. She's looking straight at me, but it's if as she's seeing through me, as if I've disappeared and she's speaking to somebody else.

'He got you, traitor, and he'll get her, too.'

I poke at Mrs Gibson, jab like a fencer with all my strength, prod her into the door frame.

'Get away from me,' I shout.

Finally, she looks at me, her body wobbling, her eyes bugging out with anger and frustration.

'You don't remember what your mum looked like, do you Maddy?'

I go to the door, ready to slam it in her face.

'Well, she's here with you now.'

Just as I reach her, Mrs Gibson smiles triumphantly, holding up the key to my room as if it's a trophy.

'You see that *nothing* in the corner, Maddy? That twirling bit of air?'

Before I can snatch the key from her hand, she closes the door and locks me in.

'That ghost is your mother, Maddy,' she shouts from the landing. 'That's Mary Deeprose – who betrayed us all.'

The storm has passed. A few leftover cloud clumps obscure the face of a round yellow moon. I haven't moved from the window since Mrs Gibson left. Haven't tried the door or even thought about a way out of here. I've done exactly what Missy said I should do – hidden myself away, not made any noise.

In the distance, lights appear, flickering between the cover of thinning hedges and bare trees. I'd totally forgotten that it's still Bonfire Night. People – some in cars, others on foot with lit torches, make their way home from the big parade in Crowham village, and the massive blaze that will burn for days.

I go to my bed, pick up the hollow book and take the letters out. The ghost follows, hovering on the floor, flat, like one of those ugly fish that lurk at the bottom of the sea. It's darker, with no twinkling – not pretty any more, not really a *she*.

Certainly not Mary Deeprose, no matter what that horrid Mrs Gibson said. How would Mrs Gibson know anything about the ghosts?

I look at the letters again, shuffle them in my hands like thin, brittle playing cards – what do they mean?

Now, because of your baby, it continues.

Your baby. That's Mary's baby, so it must be *me*. But what continues? Seeing the ghosts? Hearing noises, remembering terrible things?

I close my eyes, trying to conjure up that California clifftop.

I hear the ocean's roar, smell the tangy spray, feel the warmth of the sun on my skin, but I can't see Mum – instead, there's someone else.

A man – *the* man, dark-eyed, handsome, looming over me like a giant.

He is coming for you.

I take out my rucksack – unzip the outside pocket and find the pictures I tucked away. There's Mum – Susannah – and me in London, in California. But there's another picture of when I'm even younger, that I don't remember seeing. It must have been tucked behind one of the others in the photo frame. It looks like it was taken in California, but this was years before I moved to LA with Susannah.

I look at the back to see if there's a date, or a name.

Nothing. But it must be my real mum, Mary, on this California clifftop, with her back turned, facing out to the sea. And there's me. Smiling happily for the camera. The hand of the person taking the picture, almost out of the frame, is clutching my wrist, holding me still.

A man's hands. I can almost feel the powerful grip.

And in the top corner, is something else . . .

Wayward strands of windblown hair. Long twisting tendrils, black like Caleb's.

I tuck the picture away.

Who is this?

Devil. Demon.

Why was he with my mother?

What he feels for you is the opposite of love.

Why would he be here at Crowham after so many years?

He got you and he'll get her too.

A noise from downstairs wakes me from my daydream. The front door slams, and the security light has gone out.

I hear footsteps on the gravel, but when I look out the window I can't see anything on the lawn or driveway. There are lights on the road from Crowham, though. No cars or coaches any more – just the torches, denser than before, creating a huge bright mass.

There's music, too. Sounds, anyway – but it's not *Remember, Remember*, sung by overexcited children. It's humming and chanting, like that weird incantation Missy sang by the fire.

Through a gap in the trees I catch a glimpse of the torchbearers. They're not dressed in ordinary clothes – no jeans and anoraks, no wellies, jumpers or hoodies. They're wearing flowing robes, the kind druids wear for the summer solstice at Stonehenge, and their heads are covered by huge, draping cowls and hoods.

Hippies, I think. Wannabe pagans. But why would they be dressed like that? This is Bonfire Night. It's all about history and politics, about kings and traitors – it's not about the sorcery or the supernatural.

I go back to the bed, gather up the letters left scattered on my duvet. I put them into their envelopes and carefully place them – along with the picture of Mary and me – inside the book, closing the cover, sealing the secrets in their makeshift tomb. I carry it to my wardrobe to hide away, but as I push aside the laundry that's still piled in a heap, my fingers uncover something – the book I took down to the refectory the day Hannah went missing. It feels warm in my hands, as if someone's just been touching it, and it smells of burning –

I turn slowly, feeling dizzy, clinging to the book as if it's a life preserver and I'm lost in a stormy sea. Is the person who brought the book still here? I look around the room, put my ear to the locked door, peek into the bathroom, check the window, as if the creature from the basement might be hiding behind the dormer, hunkering down on all fours.

Outside, it's still dark. Tiny spots of light – the torches – glow in the distance like fireflies. The grey flattened ghost is at my feet, sluicing across the floor, back and forth, back and forth – at least I'm not totally alone.

I sit on my bed. The rich leather cover gleams, but I still can't read the title – the gold lettering is too faint. I hold the book to the lamp, turning it one way, then the other until finally, the gold seem to brighten. I can make out letters – C, O, W, M, T – and finally, words, a title.

The Crowham Martyrs

With trembling fingers, I open the book and thumb through pages, glancing at pictures I've already seen.

The forest clearing. The woman tied to a stake.

A bonfire in the woods.

Suddenly, I remember the crackling sound I heard on the phone to Hannah. And her voice. *Dark. Trees.*

Something in my stomach twists as I turn the page. The little boy near a mountain of flame – *sacrifice of the deuills childe.*

The knot inside me tightens. A young woman, a child. I think of Hannah and Jordan. Is this the terrible danger Caleb meant?

I flick back to the picture of the burning woman, the one whose name had been scratched out. I lift the book back up to the light. I look more closely at those words on the page. *Crwhm* – that must be Crowham. There's the word starting with the letter *w* and the date ending with *1515*.

But what's the name? *Alice D—*

I hold the page vertically, turn it around so that the scraped surface faces the light. I inch the paper as close to the bulb as I dare. There! Pale outlines, invisible letters etched on to the paper. *D–e–e–p–r–o–*

Finally, I can make out the entire line.

Crowham, Sussex. 5 November. 1515. Alice Deeprose, Witch.

I know who you are, Mr Casey said.

Tears sting my eyes. All the things I heard, those foul smells, the terrible fear, so strong I could taste it – they happened to someone who was real, to a woman who must be related to me . . .

Our kind. Is that what Mum – Susannah – meant? Our kind. Are we like Alice? Are we condemned to die?

I hear Caleb's voice again. *Maybe it won't be too late.*

But it is too late – too late for my murdered mother, far too late for poor Alice Deeprose.

I look again at the pictures, rubbing my fingers over the cloaked, hooded figures who drag a terrified child to the fire and watch innocent women burn, while in the shadows a handsome demon smiles with delight. I read the name again, the date –

Something slips out from the book – torn strips of paper that float to the floor.

Another letter?

No. The paper is too old, too brittle. I pick it up by one corner, afraid it will fall apart in my hands.

The strange square-ish letters, the old-fashioned words – I'm hardly able to make them out, but I've seen some of them before. On my laptop screen. On the table in the basement. But how is that possible?

My fingers do tremble as I write these words.

I pick up another piece. It's even more faded, harder to read.

Mine own brave sister—oh, lamentable childe—to be treated thus. Like to a criminal for all thy goodness. Like to an evil witch for all thy innocence.

I reach for the tiniest scrap.

5 November. 1515
A.D.

A.D. Alice Deeprose? Is this an account of how she died? Is there more? I carefully leaf through the book's pages, until I find another fragment, more yellow and fragile than the others. I hold it to the light, but can only make out the first few words . . .

The . . . devil . . . liveth . . . in . . . yonder . . . woods.

Yonder woods. Devil.

The devil liveth . . .

The book slips from my fingers and crashes to the floor. I rush to the window, put my face up to the glass. Where have they gone – the people dressed up like the crowds in the pictures?

I see the torches moving, but not along the road to the village – they're going into Crowham Wood, towards the centre of the forest.

Suddenly, another light flashes, directly below my window. Two torch-carrying figures hurry down the drive-way. One looks like a grown-up, but the other's just little. As they reach the gates, they stop, and the small one turns around and looks up at me. The torchlight shines on his face and for a fraction of a second – before he's pulled away, disappearing into the darkness – I see who it is.

Darshan.

Dark. Trees.

Hannah. Jordan. Darshan.

The devil liveth in yonder woods.

I stay still, clutching the windowsill, trying to control my panicky breaths. All around me, it's quiet. There's just me and the ghost who's shimmying up the wall, brightening the dark corner near the window, lovely and shiny again.

But not my mum. It can't be, can it?

I go to the door. Still locked from the outside.

I have to get out – I have to learn the truth about what's happened to my friends, no matter how horrible it is, before it's too late.

Keep quiet, Missy said, *stay hidden in the attic where it's safe.*

I back away from the door, pick the fireplace poker off the floor.

He got you and he'll get her, too.

Fine, I think. *Come and get me – man or monster, whatever you are – I'll be ready.*

I hold the poker with two hands, ready to bash the door down, feeling the anger, and the power that's flowing through my body.

But then I remember – everyone's back from the bonfire. All

the girls are downstairs, asleep. If I make a noise, somebody's bound to hear it, bound to get Missy or Mrs Gibson to check up on me.

But I can't leave my friends on their own. I can't let them be sacrificed in the woods like Alice Deeprose.

I hear a scratching behind me.

The ghost. She – it – is twirling in a tight circle, so fast it looks like a tiny ball of light. And suddenly the strange power in my body strengthens – something electric jolts my muscles, courses through my veins.

I take the door handle, and pull with all my might.

No good.

I think about Alice Deeprose, those pictures in the devil book, the laughing, leering man . . .

The anger gets stronger, I feel it boiling inside me. I pull again on the handle, with both hands this time.

I think of Mary Deeprose. I hear the sound of her laughter, I feel on my skin the gentleness of her touch.

I pull at the door again, planting my feet firmly on the floor.

A creak of metal, a cracking of wood.

I think of my friends – Hannah, Jordan, Darshan – of darkness and trees. I smell the flames, feel their terror.

No, I think. *I won't let you hurt them.*

I pull and pull on the door, as the sounds in my head get

louder and louder – so many angry cries, such terrible screaming – until the night air outside my room is shaken with thunder. The walls tremble, too, as if there's been a tiny earthquake. I hear the windows rattle, feel the floor sway gently under my feet, as the door frame shifts and the handle squeaks.

I step back from the door. Whoa. What was all that? That rush through my body, my head, my hands?

Where is your power?

That's what Mrs Gibson said. But she meant Mum, didn't she? She didn't mean me, she couldn't have meant . . .

It continues.

What continues? What *exactly?*

I try the door again, feel the pulse in my fingertips.

I turn the handle, and it opens.

Like a miracle.

Like magic.

41

Mrs Gibson must be on night watch. She stands in front of the blazing fire in the entrance hall, her arms held out at her side. There's a chair in the centre of the marble floor and a flask and some sandwiches on the reception desk.

I watch from the top of the stairs, clutching the fireplace poker. I count the number of steps, try to figure out how fast I'll have to run to beat Mrs Gibson to the doorway. Her reflexes can't be that great, and it looks as if she's in a proper trance, like Missy was when I heard her sing that weird song.

As I creep toward the bottom of the stairs, the boards creak under my feet, but Mrs Gibson doesn't turn around – she must be going deaf.

Another few steps, almost halfway down. Mrs Gibson hasn't moved, or even twitched. It's like she's been turned into a statue made of dull, grey stone. And her arms are still outstretched. How can she hold them out for so long? Who'd have guessed she'd have the strength?

I'm at the bottom of the stairs. The fire crackles and blazes. Mrs Gibson's totally still. She isn't even swaying slowly, like Missy did. What's going on?

I'm at the door, my heart pounding, that tingling power in my veins subsiding.

I turn around one last time. From this angle, I can see Mrs Gibson's face. She should be able to see me, too, but she just gazes upwards with unblinking eyes.

I unlatch the lock, open the door. A cold wind rushes in, tinkling the glass on the chandelier, feeding the flames on the fire.

Mrs Gibson still doesn't move.

Is this another miracle? Is it more magic? Who has done this?

No time to find out.

From the doorway, I can make out the torches in the forest, and smell smoke from the fires. Even though the sky is cloudy and dull, the night seems alive with electricity – the whole world seems filled with the mad pulse I felt between me and Caleb, that tingling power that surges through my muscles and my blood.

I step on to the flagstone steps, and close the door. The light from the fire glows through the windows on either side and that's when I see them – deep slashes in the mortar, claw-marks like the ones in Crowham village.

The sign of the monster? A sign that he's here?

I tear down the damp gravel driveway, swinging the poker, slicing the air.

I cross Crowham Road and follow the soft shoulder, looking into the woods for the path that Hannah and I took that night.

Suddenly, lights appear from around a bend in the road. A car's head lamps.

I hunch down and retreat into the scrubby brush beside the road. After the car passes, I scramble up a low embankment, using the poker to help stay balanced.

I slip behind a tree, breathless. The damp earth under my feet smells of mould and musty leaves, but there's a patch of bare dirt in front of me that might be a path. I turn around and look across the road at the school gates, one last time.

I step into the forest.

There's a long furrow dug into the centre of the path, with rough footprints on either side, as if someone's been dragged along between two people. Soon it veers off the trail, disappearing into the undergrowth. I follow, kicking aside a thick cluster of thorny brush. I cover my face with the sleeve of my jacket and duck to avoid hitting my head on a low-hanging branch. I keep moving, sloshing through mud, crunching on dead twigs and tree limbs, catching my feet on brambles and roots.

Finally, I reach a clearing where I can stand and catch my breath. From somewhere in the forest there's a deep chant, like the droning of a million bees. It must be those people in hoods – I must be getting closer.

Above me the black sky has cleared. It's studded with stars, and a gauzy veil of smoke wafts across the treetops. I can smell it, too – a fire burning nearby. I listen carefully – can I hear the crackle? The hollow flutter of leaping flames?

No.

I hear something else, though.

Growling – the same sound I heard in the basement.

I clutch my makeshift sword in front of me, plant my feet in the dirt. I take deep breaths, trying to stop the panic that's rising in my chest, clouding my thoughts, making me want to scream and shout. Someone is close to me – some*thing*.

A raspy breath fills the darkness. 'I know you're here.'

I stay completely still – my heart is beating so fast I'm afraid I'll die if I breathe. So much for magic, so much for having powers or being brave.

'I knew you'd come, Madeline.'

Madeline. My heart catches in my throat. *He knows my name.*

The wind rattles the dry branches above my head, and I hear the chanting again. An amber light spreads into the dark fringe of forest and the scent of burning wood seeps into the fabric of my clothes.

But the man is silent – has he gone?

I creep forward, taking faltering steps towards the light until I reach a gap in the trees. Torchlight filters through the branches. It looks exactly like the pictures in the book. Figures in long robes and hooded cloaks – there must be dozens of people – sway and chant in front of a smouldering bonfire that explodes into life as a circle is formed around it.

Are they anything to do with the growling man?

Of course, they are, I think, as I sink to the ground, dizzy with fear, and crouch behind a shrubby thicket. They *have* to be.

I can't see anything from where I'm hiding, but I can still hear the weird chanting, the hissing and snapping of flames, my own thumping heart. And rising above all these other sounds, is something even more dreadful.

It's the sound of a child, sobbing with fear.

42

I creep as close to the edge of the forest as I dare. Maybe a hood will slip, or I'll see a face or a strand of hair, some way to work out who these people are, and what they're doing. Maybe one of them will move out of the way, so I can see who is crying.

A figure – straight-backed, graceful – steps out of the circle, approaches the fire and bows before adding a piece of wood. As the others follow in turn, each adding fuel to the flames, a thought flashes through my mind, sears into my vision.

I've seen this before, and not just in books or dreams. I've peered into the hollow spaces where people's faces should be, I've heard the droning chants and the heart-breaking sobs, I've smelled the acrid smoke and felt the heat of the flames singeing hair, burning clothes, melting skin.

We know who you are.

The world spins. I lean against a tree, hugging the solid, thick trunk for support. The horrific sounds I heard in Mr Casey's history lesson weren't fantasies, they were flashbacks. Recovered memories of something in the past.

I have been here before.

I've watched women die in fear and agony – they have been my mothers, my sisters, they have been *me*. I've felt their blood in my veins – I feel it now – the tingling armour that's been passed from Alice Deeprose to Mary – my mother – and finally to me.

Madeline Deeprose.

A stiff wind blows across the clearing and the fire climbs to wilder heights. Through tiny gaps in the circle, I see another figure, smaller than the others, creep into the centre. With one hand he carries a twig, holding it out like he's roasting marshmallows and, with the other hand, pulls back the drooping folds of a sleeve. He hurls the twig with a thin brown arm, stumbles on his way back to the circle. There's a bandage on his tiny wrist – it must be Darshan.

I want to shout out to him to run away, but someone pulls him back into the circle, adjusts his hood, helps him get back into the monotonous swaying, the ominous chanting.

Why has he been brought here?

I think about that picture in the books. *The sacrifice of the deuill's childe.* It looks the same – the looming figures, the terrified kid. I turn around, peer into the forest. Is there a demon, too, smiling in the shadows, dark and handsome like the man in my dreams?

In the clearing, the circle widens, spreading towards the fringe of the forest, closer to me, within touching distance of the tree I'm clinging to. The chanting stops so all I hear is the wind whispering through the trees, rustling the robes of the people in hoods, fanning the fire's angry flames. In the distance – it sounds so odd and out of place here – traffic hums on Crowham Road.

I hear the crying again – but it's not Darshan. Another child-sized figure stands shakily between the swaying circle and the hissing flames. As it peers up at the fire, its hood slips back. I take a deep breath, putting my fist to my mouth to stop myself from shouting out.

It's Jordan. And who's that beside him, arms wrapped tightly around his bony shoulders?

It has to be Hannah.

I remember Caleb's words. *Maybe it's not too late.*

But how can I stop this? Even if I distracted the crowd – if I shouted at the top of my lungs or rushed into the centre of the circle and started pulling at their hoods – would Jordan, Darsh and Hannah have time to break free and escape?

I lean against the tree and face the forest.

The darkness tempts me. On the other side of these trees is

safety, it says. You can run for help. You can race into Crowham and tell everyone that there's a mob of crazy people who are about to throw your friends on to a bonfire. The police will come, ambulances will arrive.

Jordan's crying gets louder.

I turn back to the circle. Hannah's comforting him, telling him not to be afraid, promising that he'll be fine as long as he does as he's told . . .

Another figure steps out of the circle, turns towards me as I inch back behind the tree. It holds out its arms, pointing in my direction, as if it knows where I'm hiding.

My heart sinks as he lifts his head. Even though I can't see his face, I sense Caleb's bright eyes, burning into me the way they did the night I first saw him, and I feel the pulse, the pull.

Maybe it's not too late. I hear his voice, as clearly as if he were whispering in my ear.

As the heat of the flames reddens my cheeks and Caleb gazes into the forest, searching me out, I understand the truth – part of it, anyway.

These people, swaying and chanting – whoever they are, whatever terrible things they mean to do in this clearing, they don't want to do them to Jordan or Hannah or Darshan.

I remember what it said in the letters to my mother.

When our kind die, his kind die too.

I know who these people really want to destroy.

Our kind.

Me.

I take a deep breath. I push through the barrier of the circle and stumble into the light of the fire.

43

'Here I am.'

The chanting stops. No one moves. It's as if my words have turned them into statues.

Across the clearing, Hannah gawps, open-mouthed. Her skin looks grey and dull as she stares vacantly at Jordan, who's huddled in her arms. I look for Darshan – he's still in the circle, clutching the hands of the people standing beside him.

And what about Caleb? Has he retreated into the anonymity of the crowd?

'Let Hannah and Darshan and Jordan go,' I say, holding my arms out imploringly.

Still no movement or acknowledgement. Can't they see me? Don't they understand? Am I invisible?

'It's me. Madeline Deeprose. The one you want.' My voice rises, straining to be heard. 'So stop this.'

My words echo around the clearing, and the surrounding trees shake. The bonfire's timber support shifts suddenly, and sparks shoot out like fireworks.

But nothing else – nobody – moves.

I stomp my foot. 'Let them go!'

The ground trembles again, and the fire rages, but the figures don't budge.

I step closer to my friends. 'Hannah?'

Why doesn't she answer? Why doesn't she move?

I move around the clearing. The silence is more frightening than any sound – has everybody been put under a spell, like Mrs Gibson seemed to be?

Hannah's eyes are closed and Jordan's are glazed over. I check on Darshan, lifting the heavy cloth that hides his face. His eyes are lifeless and staring. And who's that beside, him, I wonder, still clutching his hand? I reach to pull back the hood, but something stops me.

The growling is back.

My heart leaps higher than the flames. Is the monster here – somewhere in the circle? For a second I think about running a way – the woods are all around me, and beyond them are roads and cars and villages – but another sound keeps me glued to the spot.

A single, spoken word.

'Madeline.'

Cloth rustles. I turn to the sound, and see something –

someone – stir. At first it's just a flick of the head, and another swoosh of cloth. Then it's a step. And another one, out of the circle. And another, until a figure is standing between me and the fire.

I wait for the next move, knowing who it will be – who it *must* be – as two hands are raised and the heavy concealing cloth is pushed back.

Dark hair tumbles out, reflecting the firelight, gleaming like a helmet of ebony or onyx. The face is beautiful – blue eyes, heavy lashes, full mouth, square chin, strong, chiselled jaw –

It's him. The man from my visions. The man who pulled me along the clifftop in my nightmares. The man who killed my mother.

He's alive, exactly as I dreamed him. He's real; he's here.

'I know who you are,' I say.

He moves closer, looms over me. 'Do you?'

I hold my head high, as if I'm not scared, but my hands are clasped behind my back so he won't see them shake.

'You murdered my mother.'

He smiles. Perfect white teeth glint in the light of the fire.

'I saw you. On that clifftop, when I was little – I was there.'

'Yes,' he says, his voice is wheezy, as if his lungs are full of rust. 'You were.'

The fire shifts again, a spark flashes out, hot embers sting my skin. My eyes fill with tears, but I don't – *I won't* – flinch or cry out. Instead, I grit my teeth and stand up tall, planting my feet firmly on the ground.

'What are you waiting for?' I sneer. 'You've got the fire ready, you've put everyone in some weird trance, so why are you wasting your time?'

'Why indeed.' The man strides towards me as I take another look into the forest, desperate to find some magical way of escaping – a time portal, a flying carpet, St Michael and his angels, an army of ghosts . . .

His powerful hands are clasped around my waist, burning me like the flames they're pulling me towards. As the heat of the fire gets stronger, I try to break away, kicking out, lashing at the man's body with my feet and hands, but he's too strong, and his grip on me is too –

Shout, child. A voice inside my head is speaking – who is that? *Tremble the earth with thine anger!*

'Stop it!' I cough and sputter – it's not enough.

My lungs burn, I can hardly breathe, but I have to try once more, before it's all –

Closer and closer to the flames – and still no one is able to help me, still all voices are silent except the one that is speaking inside me, as the man who is *more monstrous than the reste* drags me to the fire.

44

I gaze into the forest – from whence comes my salvation? From whence my liberty? Oh thou, my brother, who stands speechless and amazed, wilt thou not tell them, 'My sister must not be slain'? And thou, my most beloved sisters, art thou afeared to speak of mine innocence?

Behold how the monster laughs and jeers at my suffering, how he hideth himself away in the belly of the woods – the wretched devilish coward.

Oh, I am drawn too close to escape now. I feel the burning – I know this will be a piteous end – but am I afraid? No.

Behold your sister. Does she quiver before the fire?

No. The fire grows higher, the flames lash at her skin, but does your sister cry out?

I hear the answer in my head.

No!

I shriek it at the top of my lungs. 'No!'

The man pushes me. At first I think I've landed in the

flames – I choke, my skin screams with imagined pain – but I've merely been slung in front of the fire like a bag of rubbish.

I roll away from the heat, try to stand again, to gather my strength and courage. If I have to die in this horrible place, I want to face it on two feet – defiant like my mother, as brave as Alice Deeprose.

It's no use – I'm totally out of breath, and too exhausted to even lift my head.

But there's another voice in the clearing.

I lay still and listen. Am I dreaming? Am I already dead?

Somewhere between the raging fire and the hard ground, there's a harsh human whisper, followed by a nasty snarl.

'Was her mother not enough for you?

I push myself up to see.

The human voice is Caleb's. He and the man are facing off, their hands gripped together, their robes skirting the edge of the flames. The man opens his mouth, but there are no words. There's just the growling, just the raspy breath.

'And was *my* mother not enough?'

A bitter howl replies.

'And now, Father –'

Father? What? This man, this murdering monster, can't be his . . .

'– and now you want to take Maddy as well?'

As I inch backwards, the man looks at me and smiles. He's Caleb's double – I see it now. Of course that's his father.

'If you hurt Maddy,' Caleb says, 'what will you gain?'

The man doesn't answer. There's no sound at all – the wind has stopped rustling the tops of the trees, the fire has stopped crackling.

'You know who she is, don't you?' Caleb asks.

The man moves towards me, but Caleb steps in front of him, blocking his path.

'Maddy could make you stronger,' Caleb shouts. 'Don't you understand? What good would it do to hurt her . . . to harm your own . . .'

A rumble deep under the ground muffles the sound of Caleb's terrible word.

I put my hands up to my ears, so I won't hear what he's saying, but it's too late –

'Your own daughter?'

The word hangs in the air like a foul stench.

I scramble to my feet, stagger towards the fire. 'Why are you saying this, Caleb?' My lungs burn, my throat's closing up, but I have to speak. 'Why are you telling these terrible –'

'My own sister?'

I stop dead.

The monster smiles again. He speaks to me in a human voice. 'So now you know the truth.'

I shake my head. No. I don't know. This is *not* the truth – none of it!

'Daughter,' he says.

He looks at Caleb, shaking his hair so it shines like snakeskin. 'Son.'

I stare beyond them into the fire, where the flames dance and strut. I see something else, too. *Remember, remember.* The man – this murderer – at the top of the cliff.

My mother backing away.

Run, Maddy!

The man standing still, reluctant to follow her, as if he knows it's a trick.

Run, Maddy, run!

Mum backing closer and closer to the edge of the cliff, trying to protect me, trying to lure the man away from –

Mum falling.

I open my eyes. Feel the heat of the flames on my face.

The man did not want her to die that day.

It was the same then, as it is now – the one he really wanted to kill was me.

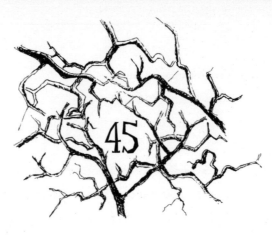

45

'Maddy! Look out!'

Caleb screams as the man breaks away from his grasp, and crosses the clearing in long graceful strides, grabbing my shoulders, dragging me closer to the fire.

With one hand he tilts my head, examines my face, touches my hair. My eyes glaze over, and his painful grip is all that keeps me from collapsing on to the ground. I'm too weak to scream, too exhausted to kick or hit.

I look up at the handsome face, stare straight into those dazzlingly blue eyes, eyes that are flecked with spots of green and gold. Just like Caleb's. Just like mine.

I smile at him like an obedient child – *his* obedient child.

'Daughter,' he says, and I spit in his face.

He staggers back – even murderers must feel disgust – and as he wipes his cheek, struggling to regain his balance, Caleb rushes forward and pushes him to the ground, straddling his chest.

'Run, Maddy!' Caleb screams.

The ground shivers. So Caleb can do it, too – make the earth move by the power of his feelings.

'Now!'

Caleb's face is damp with sweat, red with the reflection of the fire, as the man beneath him twists and slithers like a serpent under St Michael's feet. The man cries out with rage – a terrible, howling hiss – behind me people move, and the chanting starts again.

While others in the circle sway, a figure steps forward, raises a hand, pulls back her hood.

It's Missy, her eyes fluttering blankly, back and forth.

'What are you doing, Missy?' I shout. 'With these people – with *him?*'

The man snarls like an animal, flailing his arms, trying to gather his strength.

'You've got to go, Maddy,' Caleb shrieks. 'Get out of the forest and back to your room.'

Another woman steps forward. My heart sinks as she reveals her face – Reverend Anne. Kind, sweet Reverend Anne. She stares at the fire with steely determination. What are these women planning to do? Burn me at the stake? Or abandon me to my fate like Alice Deeprose?

As the circle inches closer I see the faces beneath the hoods.

Some I recognise from the village – the librarian, the newsagent, the man who's always outside the pub smoking. The rest are from the school – teachers, caretakers, Mr Grayling's PA.

Finally, another person steps into the clearing, arms outstretched. Even before she pushes the cloth from her face, I know who she'll be.

'Mum?'

No, that silent, stony-faced woman is not my mother. She's not even *Susannah,* she's no one, just another soulless minion, here to . . .

'Hurry, Maddy,' Caleb cries. 'Go with the others.'

Through a gap in the circle I see that Hannah, Darshan and Jordan have broken free. They're sheltering in a cluster of trees. All around them, swirling over their heads and between their bodies, is a patch of silvery, ghostly light.

'There's still time for you to get out of here, before . . .'

'Before what?'

'Just go, Maddy.'

'What do they want to do to me?'

'It's not *you* they're after, Maddy.' Caleb shakes his head. 'Don't you understand?'

He looks down at the man, then raises his head and nods at the fire. 'I don't want you to see this.'

As the circle closes in, as the chanting grows louder, more

terrifying, I realise what Caleb means. It's not *me* they want to kill, it's not me they want to throw on to the fire. It's the man – the howling thing who calls himself my father.

'No,' I say. 'You can't.'

Caleb groans, breathless with exhaustion. 'He murdered my mother. He killed yours, too.'

'But we'd be doing the same – we'd be no better.'

Caleb laughs, in spite of his exertion. 'But he's not *human*, Maddy. Can't you see?'

The fire flares up, huge and roaring, as if someone has stoked it with fresh wood and fanned the angry flames. The man beneath Caleb pants, kicks and scratches. Then he stops, as if his rage has exhausted him. His huge, gleaming eyes catch mine – they're full of fear, sorrow, regret, and all I feel for him is pity.

I shake my head. 'He's a man, Caleb. Human, like you, like me, whatever he's done.'

'Look again, Maddy. See what's underneath.'

A quick glance is all I need, but I have to blink to make sure it's real.

Before my eyes the man has become what I imagined and feared, what Jordan saw, what Hannah could sense – a demon, with evil, bulging eyes, and small twisted horns that poke through the top of his shell-like skull.

'Madeline, my darling,' the creature growls. He reaches for

287

me with leathery hands, scratches my legs with brittle claws.

'So now you know,' Caleb sighs.

I stumble backwards, too dazed with horror to speak. Is this what everyone knew about me? This creature – *devil, demon* – is my father?

And these people who I thought were my teachers, my friends – Missy, Reverend Anne, Caleb – have they come together in this strange place to kill him?

'Get out of here, Maddy,' Caleb groans. 'Or help us do what has to be done.'

I look around the clearing. Missy and the others stare at the flames, their chants growing louder, stronger. The monster scowls and grimaces, hissing like a snake as Caleb's grip on him weakens.

'Am I meant to push him on to the fire?' I shriek. 'Do you want to burn him alive?'

I look beyond the clearing – as if the forest could give me the answer. The ghostlight still shines through the trees, bigger and brighter than before. As I gaze on it, a feeling washes over me like a powerful wave, overturning the confusion, sweeping aside the disgust and fear, filling me with a conviction that's as solid and unbending as St Michael's sword.

I turn back to Caleb.

'He mustn't die.'

I look at the creature on the ground, who pants like the slavering dog we saw in the wood, and howls with blood-curdling desperation.

'Not here. Not like –'

Missy and Reverend Anne step forward. 'But you can help us,' Missy shouts.

'No,' I say. 'I can't help you – I *won't* – not this way.'

'Do you want to die, Maddy?' Caleb shouts, as the monster kicks and twists beneath him, gathering strength.

'I'm not meant to *kill*. I know that.'

'Think about your mother,' Caleb whispers.

I look at the light in the forest – glowing like an Earth-bound moon. And beside it is a shimmering star, my beautiful ghost . . .

'I *am* thinking of her.'

I look into Caleb's eyes – so much like this horrible creature's – and I see my own face reflected there.

'There has to be another way.'

'We must be rid of him,' Missy shouts. 'There's no other way.'

'There *is*,' I say.

I hold out my hand to Caleb, and feel the strange energy flowing between us, strengthening my resolve.

'We're more powerful than he is,' I say. 'Don't you understand that? Can't you feel it? The two of us together – if we really

289

are brother and sister, we have to be.'

As my hand inches closer to Caleb, the pulse increases. The ghost cloud sweeps out of the forest and into the clearing, cooling the air, damping down the flames.

So this is what it means to be a Deeprose, I think. So this is *who I am.*

'If you truly are my brother, then trust me, please.'

The creature twitches and snarls but, at last, Caleb stands up and joins me. As the monster clambers to its feet, Caleb pulls his robe over his head and kicks it away. In jeans and T-shirt he looks like a normal boy, but as he takes my hand the energy flows through my veins like thick blood, hardening into armour.

The demon creeps towards us. His face is dark purple, his singed brows turn downward. Caleb tightens his grip on my hand.

'Stay inside the circle, Maddy,' he whispers. 'It will keep us safe.'

The monster leans into me, and touches my face, gently somehow. His eyes, so like Caleb's, so like mine, are as beautiful as any I've ever seen –

'Come with me,' he murmurs, in his gurgling language that I can suddenly understand.

'Don't look at him.' Caleb whispers. 'He tried this with

me – don't trust him, Maddy.'

'I never wanted you to die, my darling Madeline,' the creature coos. 'I only wanted –'

'No,' I say.

'I only wanted to love you.'

Caleb squeezes my hand with all his might, but I feel another power, almost as strong as the one we share, pulling me away from him, dragging my heart towards the man, towards the fire.

No, I think, closing my eyes, turning them away from the hideous creature and his beautiful lies. *Remember . . .*

The earth sways as images flash through my mind – the shining faces of Alice Deeprose's sobbing sisters and broken-hearted brother who watch her die, the hard frosty ground beneath her bare feet, the executioners' soulless eyes as she is dragged towards them, the swinging rope, creaking against the rough timber frame – the searing, soaring flames. And at the edge of the forest, beyond her vision, but not beyond mine – someone lurks, with burning eyes and a jeering grin. This man, my father, the one that is *more monstrous than the reste* – watches with glee, laughs at her pain.

'Madeline. My darling.'

I open my eyes. The burning timber shifts. 'Didn't you hear me?'

As I speak, the fire rises up again, belching out smoke and flame, shooting sparks across the dark sky. 'I said *no*.'

When I look again the monster is human – tall, dark, beautiful – but beneath the skin I see a scaly hide, and behind his bright blue eyes, there's a dead, yellow tinge.

'No more lies,' I say, as the trees bend and sway.

The man turns his mouth up – as if that smile could draw me in, as if his tainted beauty could sway me like it did my poor murdered mother.

'Go,' Caleb says, and the earth does a little dance, shimmying under our feet.

Hannah, Jordan and Darshan come back to the circle as it tightens around us like a protective cloak, and the man steps back, growling. He slouches, hunching his shoulders, dropping his arms as his body lowers and he becomes a creature again. He leans towards me with his red face, still so sure of his charisma, his strength, his power to control and deceive –

'Now!' I shout.

As the trees shiver and the ground rumbles, the monster lopes towards the forest. He looks back at me . . . once, twice . . . as if he can't believe what has happened. He trips over a vine, recovers, straightens.

He stumbles one last time, time before vanishing, defeated, into the dark.

46

The ghost is hiding under my bed. She's grey-white, translucent – not silvery or shimmery any more. Maybe it's not the same one. Maybe it's not *mine*.

I pull off my damp clothes, slip into a dry t-shirt and tracksuit bottoms. As I fall into bed I hear footsteps on the stairs outside, but I'm too tired to be scared.

'Maddy?' Mum's voice.

I turn around and face the wall. I don't want to see anybody, especially not her, but it's not just Mum. It's all of them, the whole Crowham Martyrs posse – Mum, Missy, Reverend Anne.

'Please, darling, just listen to what we have to say . . .'

Mum – Susannah, that is – sits on the edge of the bed. She touches my hair and runs a finger along my cheek. 'The things we've done – the lies – we only did them because we were so frightened.'

I sit up, turn to face her. 'Who's this *we* you keep talking about?'

'Us,' she says, waving her arm towards the other women. 'Your aunts.'

I look around the room, studying Reverend Anne's worried frown, Missy's satisfied smile, Mum's bright eyes, shiny with tears.

'My *aunts*?'

Reverend Anne steps forward. 'We're your mother's sisters, Maddy. We wrote the letters you found. We're the Deeproses – Elizabeth, Anne, Susannah.'

'And Mary?' I say. 'Who was she?'

Mum smiles, nods, brushes away the tear that rolls down her cheek. 'Mary was the best of us.'

Mum brings me hot chocolate and tells the story of our *special family*, as she calls it, rabbiting on about things that have been happening since the dawn of time.

'I already know this stuff,' I snap. 'I saw the books, I remembered those horrible times – saw Alice Deeprose in my visions. So what are we, anyway? Witches?'

Mum shuts up in mid jaw-flap. Reverend Anne clucks like a strangled hen.

'Most of the powerful magic died out ages ago,' Missy says.

294

'We can still perform protection spells when we need – like the one that kept your room safe and the one in the forest that kept the circle safe, for a while – but the more dramatic tricks have gone by the wayside, sadly.'

I look her in the eyes. 'Not for me.'

There's a flicker of fear in Missy's face, but for once, she seems lost for words.

'The rumbling in the woods,' Mum whispers, as if it needed explaining.

'What is that?' I ask.

Mum shakes her head. 'We don't know. We think it might come from –'

Missy butts in again, angrily spitting her words. 'From *him*.'

'We can *see* things, that's all,' Mum says. 'What others can't. What people actually look like under the skin. And we remember what so many others won't. The horrors you saw, the noises you heard, all the terrible things that have happened through the ages.'

'And today,' Reverend Anne adds. 'Right now. The world is still full of cruelty, we must remember that, too . . .'

Missy continues the story. All about how the Deeprose women had to be careful – choose partners wisely, in case *he*, or someone like him, charmed them into falling in love and losing their hearts – and themselves – to a monster. Missy took a job at the school, Anne become a priest and married Tom, who already had children, and Susannah moved around, never settling in one place.

'It was only Mary – your birth mother – who wasn't careful,' Missy says. 'Only Mary who ran off with a man she fell totally, madly in love with.'

I feel that strange pull again – as if the word 'love' is tugging at my heart. Mum takes my hand, squeezes it the way Caleb did when we were standing in front of our father.

'Why couldn't she see the demon side of him, like I did?'

'They say love is blind.' Reverend Anne's voice is tight and heavy. She turns away, wiping her eyes. 'That must have been it.'

'Who is he?' I ask. 'Is he, like, a real person – does he have a name?

There's a terrible silence, and Mum looks around anxiously, as if he might have slipped into the room with us – invisible, undetected.

'I have the right to know, don't I?'

'Of course you do, my darling,' Mum coos, pawing my fingers.

'His name is James Thorne,' Missy says. 'That's what he calls himself anyway, but who knows if it's true. Deeprose? Thorne? Seems a horrid joke.'

Mum moves closer, clutching my hand. 'We knew what

he was, long before poor Mary did.'

'So he's a devil? Like in the pictures?'

Missy takes a deep breath. 'He's not an actual devil,' she says, 'any more than you're a witch. But he was once – at least his kind were – and what you saw was the truth, the essence, of him. His kind thrives on cruelty, injustice, the suffering of others. They laugh at it – exactly like the creature you saw in the pictures. They do what they can to spoil the world, to create conflict and hatred where there should be beauty and love. And they get away with it, too, because nobody sees what they're really like . . .'

'Except us?'

'And those who are similar to us, those who help. They know what we do, but they don't see things as clearly – the Mr Caseys and the Mrs Gibsons of this world.'

'Mrs Gibson's a helper?' I pull a face. 'But she's been horrible to me – she called my mother a traitor, she came after me with a poker, she said some terrible things.'

Missy smiles. 'Yes, that *was* a tad harsh – she was only meant to have checked up on you – but Mrs Gibson's always been a stickler for the rules, and sometimes her over-zealous nature takes things too far.'

Mum steps in again. 'Hannah's parents realised their daughter was one, too – one of our helpers – so they sent her here so we could keep her safe. Darshan and Jordan, as well – what Jordan called *fings* are the evil spirits that still lurk about. They're both too young to understand any of this yet, though.'

'So where did you take my friends when I thought they'd been kidnapped?'

'Jordan and Hannah were taken to the vicarage,' Missy says. 'For their own protection.'

'But I was there – looking for Hannah.' My throat tightens with anger when I think of that day – all those nights of worry and fear. 'And you just *lied –*'

'Once you found the books, we had no choice,' Reverend Anne sobs. She sniffs again, wipes her nose. 'Hannah's curiosity was putting everything at risk, so we had to get her away from you; we had to stop her from getting in contact. We wiped her message from your phone, confiscated her mobile, and when she made that call from my husband's phone, we kept her . . . well . . .'

'Then why were they in the woods tonight – Hannah and Jordan and Darsh? It doesn't make sense.'

'They were safer with us than being left on their own,' Missy says. 'Just like you were safer in the attic with the magic protecting you.'

'Or would have been,' Reverend Anne says, 'if James Thorne

hadn't done a spell of his own and put poor Mrs Gibson into a trance.'

'As long as we kept your friends inside the sacred circle, inside our protection,' Mum says, 'everything should have been fine.'

I shake my head and roll my eyes. Sacred circles and secrets plans and Mrs Gibson in a trance – this all sounds so ridiculous. 'Why didn't you just tell the truth from the start? Wouldn't that have been easier?'

'Perhaps,' Missy says. 'But to tell you who your father was? To explain what we planned to do as soon as he came for you? Would you really have wanted to know?'

I don't answer. I'm so tired I can hardly think.

'And you know what happened when someone tried to tell you,' Mum cries. 'You saw with your own eyes . . .'

I shake my head. I don't want to think of poor Mr Casey, struggling to speak and to breathe.

Mum squeezes my hand. 'We thought it was the right thing, darling,' she says. Better for you. We'd have been rid of him forever, and you would never have known.'

I drink the last of my hot chocolate, yawning. Missy takes my empty cup. She and Reverend Anne hover for a few seconds, tutting and sighing, before shuffling out of my room. Only Mum – Susannah – stays.

'You understand, don't you?' she says, getting up to close the door behind them. 'We knew he'd come, Maddy. While we were in Los Angeles there were signs that he was closing in.'

She sits back down on the edge of the bed.

'Strange rumblings,' she whispers. 'We mistook them for earthquakes at first.'

'And so you sent me away . . .'

'You were growing up. Remembering things, becoming a proper Deeprose. We thought you'd be safer here, protected by our skills, and surrounded by the goodness that has been here for so long.'

Mum stops talking. Takes my hands.

'But then Thorne managed to find Caleb, so we knew it was just a matter of time. And since it was Bonfire Night and the anniversary of Alice Deeprose's . . .' She sighs wearily. "We knew he'd come for you."

'So where is he now?' I turn over to face her. 'This James Thorne. Where do you think he's gone?'

'He's been abroad for the past few years. Working in the arms trade – nasty stuff.' Mum shudders in disgust. 'But we saw him off – you and Caleb did, anyway – so, hopefully . . .'

'What makes him so dangerous to me?'

'He killed your mother –'

'That doesn't mean he wants to kill me. He said as much

tonight, he told me he didn't want to hurt me, he only wanted –'

'To love you?'

I nod, trying to ignore that tug at my heart.

'And you believed him, just like your mother did. Maybe only for a few seconds, but what if you were drawn to him – he is your father after all, and he's powerful and cunning. What if you were tricked by him – became like him?'

'So it was better to lie to me, like he did?'

Mum shakes her head

'To send me away. To keep me prisoner at Crowham, without any friends.'

'My darling, I'm so –'

'I suppose Severine and Olga leaving in Year 7 was down to you, too?'

She bites her bottom lip so I know it must be the truth.

'To leave me all on my own, when I needed you most?'

Mum puts her face into her hands and sobs. Proper crying, not the mediocre actress kind. Real tears, actual snot.

'And to lie about Caleb –'

'Nobody lied,' she sighs.

I shake my head with astonishment. 'I have a brother, and you never told me?

'How could we, Maddy? That would have meant telling you about your father and that was something we wanted never to do, something we hoped we wouldn't have to.'

I lie down, turn away from her again.

'All these things were to keep you safe, darling.' Mum whimpers and sniffs. 'We did everything because we love you so much.'

It's dark – Mum must have turned out the light. She's sleeping on the floor, the top half of her body draped across my bed. And in the window, sparkly and pretty again, almost as dazzling as the light I saw in the forest, is the ghost.

'Mum? Wake up.'

Mum yawns, stretches, opens her eyes.

'Can you see that, Mum?'

'Of course, Maddy.'

She perches on the edge of the bed and I let her hold me in her arms while the ghost turns, a tiny planet on its own axis.

'I like this one,' I whisper. 'She's special.'

The ghost slips through a crack beneath the window and disappears into the night air. Mum and I get up, peer out into the darkness, watch her blaze across the sky – fast as a comet, shiny as a star, bright as an angel.

'Yes,' Mum answers. 'She always was.'

47

We tread along the forest path single file – Caleb, Hannah, me.

Caleb wants to see the woods before he leaves for London tomorrow. He's met his little sister – *moi* – and helped the Deeproses see off James Thorne, so he's going back to his old school, his old life with *his* mum's sister.

So far, everything's the same – muddy footprints, dense shrubs, towering pines, a damp, smoky smell. As we get closer to the clearing, the setting sun filters through the scorched branches of leafless trees.

'So it *was* real,' I say.

Caleb steps into the clearing. He looks up at the sky, strides into the centre of the blackened circle. He's the only thing that looks any different. He's hacked his curls off, shaved his head so that his hair hugs his scalp like a bristly cap.

'*He* was definitely real,' Caleb says, kicking a half-burned log into the forest. 'So was the danger to you, to all of us really, if the Crowham circle failed to protect us, and if we hadn't been able to overpower him.'

'I still don't understand why you couldn't have told me what was going on,' I say.

'I tried, didn't I?' Hannah says. 'I made those calls from the vicarage –'

'Calls that made me think you'd been dragged into the woods by a gang of murderers, not tucked up in some cosy –'

'Is it my fault the mobile signal's so rubbish around here?' Hannah snaps. 'And then they took my phone . . .'

'You could have tried some other way.' My voice is getting louder, more strident. I can tell by Hannah's face that she's upset – we've never had a row before – but that doesn't stop my anger.

'You could have sent a message, if you'd really wanted to, you could have got through . . .'

'They never let me out of my room, Maddy,' she says. 'They locked me up – what part of that do you not understand?'

Caleb steps closer to me. 'Come on, Maddy, you're not being –'

'*Fair?*' I say, my voice straining with rage. 'Well, what about you? You knew I was freaking out about Hannah going missing, you saw it with your own eyes, so why didn't you –'

'I wanted to,' he says. 'I tried – remember? But you didn't trust me enough to listen and you weren't ready to hear'

'How could I have trusted you? You were creeping around my room! And the things you knew about made me think you were a –'

Above our heads a gust of wind whooshes the black, brittle treetops, and there's a cracking sound as a branch breaks off and is left dangling.

I look up – did I do that? I remember those feelings from last night – that *power*. I stumble off the path, move closer to Caleb.

'That was the wind,' he whispers. 'Nothing to do with you.'

'How do you know?'

He shrugs. 'For me, it's never been bad, this weird stuff. It only happens when I *need* it, when it's right. It's a good thing, Maddy, trust me.'

'And I *could* have handled the truth, no matter what Missy said – I'm handling it now, right?'

Caleb shrugs and does that wavering gesture with his hand, the one that says, 'maybe, maybe not'. Then he puts his hand on my shoulder and squeezes it. He turns me around so that I can see Hannah across the clearing. Her face is red and she's wiping away tears.

'Do you know why they really took Hannah away?' Caleb whispers.

I shake my head.

'What happened to Mr Casey, that horrible death –'

I gasp, my heart almost frozen with dread.

'– he would have done the same to her.'

I groan with horror. *He. Him.*

How could I have forgotten that night in Hannah's room? The way she wouldn't stop talking even when she struggled for breath. The way she never showed any fear, even though she knew something – someone – was trying to hurt her?

Oh, Hannah, my wonderful friend.

Caleb takes my trembling hands, and leads me across the clearing, He backs away, leaving us alone.

I take a few deep breaths. 'Hannah?'

She wipes her nose with the sleeve of her jacket. 'Yeah?'

'What I said,' I sputter. 'The way I talked, I didn't mean . . .'

I try my best not to, but I crumple into a heap of sobs. 'Sorry I talked like that, Hannah,' I blub. 'I shouldn't have taken it out on you –'

'I'm sorry, too.' Hannah sniffs. 'I wanted to tell you everything – and I tried, at the beginning. But they made me so scared, Mads – so scared for you . . .'

She gazes beyond me, into the darkening forest, her brow furrowed. Then she turns around, looking up at the glowering clouds in the sky, and down at the scorched earth below our feet.

'It's almost funny you know?' she says. "My parents realised I had this weird sense, and it terrified them. So when Reverend Anne told them about Crowham, stuck in the middle of nowhere, they thought it was the answer to their prayers, so sent me here.'

Hannah shakes her head.

'Because they thought it would be safer, right?' I say.

She's sighs theatrically and waves her arms at the burnt-out mess. When I look at her, I see that her brown eyes are twinkling beneath the tears and her mouth is curling up at the corners. She's thinking the same thing as me – I know she is.

I pick up a charred piece of wood, all that's left of last night's fire.

'That was a bad call, eh?' I say.

Hannah kicks up a pile of ashes and breaks into a huge smile. 'That was a very, very bad call.'

Caleb takes a final walk around the circle while Hannah and I hug and cry and argue about which one of us has been the stupidest – I was, no I was. When we're finally ready to go we clap our arms around each other's shoulders and drag Caleb behind us. We stagger out of the clearing, laughing and shrieking. We race down the path and tumble out of the woods.

48

I look in the mirror, admiring the new model *Madeline*.

My cheekbones are highlighted with blusher. Bright, shimmering hair – *flame red* according to the box, *sensuous devil-may-care colour* – falls against my shoulders and screams for attention. There's black eyeliner around my lids and my lashes are caked in mascara – all thanks to Mum's latest care package, an attempt to buy back my love with expensive cosmetics.

I shake my head, watch my hair come alive like the fire in the forest. I lean in closer, until my nose almost touches the mirror. My eyes seem more blue than grey now. The gold flecks are brighter, too, like tiny flaring stars.

'May I have a quick word?

Missy shouts from the bottom of the stairs. Her voice is light and bouncy, as if nothing's happened, as if the clock's been turned back to the beginning of term and there've been no bonfires in the forest, no demons or witches, no secrets or lies, no horrible truth.

'Maddy? Madeline?'

Ignore her, I think. *Maybe she'll go away.*

I button my blazer, give my hair a final flick and tousle. I check around the room but the late November shadows are empty. There aren't any ghosts clogging up the corners, no flecks of silver or wisps of white vapour. I hold still for a moment and listen – maybe they're here, but invisible. I try the window – maybe the pretty one, the *motherly* one, is hiding behind a tree or hovering in the sky. It's crazy how much I miss them, I think – how much I miss *her.*

They might come back one day, I think. If I need them again . . .

The world beyond Crowham stretches wider than before. Have I grown taller, too? I stand on tiptoes. There's the forest – the nearly-bare trees, the branches that reach like scrawny fingers from a burned-out circle somewhere in the middle. I can see the cross on the steeple of Crowham church, and in the far corner, something else reaches skyward – an ugly, metal, Triffid-like tower.

There aren't any ghosts, though . . .

Hannah thought the ghosts kept me safe from all the bad stuff. That's the reason Mum and Reverend Anne gave me, too. They said now that I know the truth about myself, things are bound to be different. We can talk about James Thorne without choking, there are no more smudges and stains on the windows and mirrors for the fings to get through, and I don't need the ghosts for protection.

But still . . . I wish they hadn't all disappeared.

There's a knock on the door. Missy glides in, carrying a small paper-wrapped parcel and a green plastic binder. It's hard not to smile as she clocks my new appearance – her eyes widen, there's a sharp intake of breath, a tiny step backwards.

'Wow,' she says, trying to sound casual and cool. 'Have you had anything pierced?'

'Not yet,' I say. 'But I'm going to Brighton again at the weekend, so who knows?'

She looks around my bedroom – the bare walls give her a shock, too. There's nothing on them except the outlines of the posters and pictures that used to be there, those reminders of California, a home I never really had.

'So, it's all change for Madeline Deeprose,' she mutters.

'I chucked everything in the skip.'

'You won't be wanting these, then.' She opens the binder, turns the stiff, plastic-coated pages. 'Pictures of when you were little. And a tiny something from Reverend Anne.'

I suppose I should thank her, but I say nothing.

'All right, young lady.' She drops the binder and the packet on my bed. 'But that trip to Brighton . . .'

'What about it?' I snap.

'Make sure you take someone with you. Hannah and some of the older boys.'

'I'll be fine on my own.'

She goes to the door, waits in the doorway. 'He'll come back,' she whispers. 'He'll try again.'

I shrug. 'Whatever. I can handle it now. Caleb and I saw him off, didn't we? '

'But Caleb's back at school in London, and when James Thorne wants something . . .'

Missy's cut off by a strange sound – a deep vibration and rattle from inside the drawer of my bedside table.

'It's your mobile,' she says. 'Over the weekend a phone mast went up between here and Crowham village – we couldn't stop them this time.'

I lean over the bed, open the drawer. This is amazing – my phone's actually ringing!

'Don't answer it,' Missy hisses. 'Please – it might be *him.*'

The rumbling stops, but the phone's light is still on when I pick it up. *Unknown caller*, it says. *Number withheld.*

'A child was no use to him. But now that you're a young woman . . .'

I pop the phone into my bag, gather my pens and exercise books.

'You need to go,' I say.

'Please be careful, darling –'

'You're not my mother,' I bark. 'So stop telling me what to do.'

Missy backs away towards the door, ashen-faced, hurt.

Suddenly I think of Mary – my real mother – and it's like she's in the room with me, telling me off. 'This is my oldest sister,' she's saying. 'Your aunt – who took you in and protected you . . .'

'Sorry, Missy,' I say.

When Missy turns around her eyes are wet with tears. She sighs and sniffs, but manages a wobbly smile.

I smile, too. Sniff just a little. 'And I'll be really careful, so don't worry, okay?'

I take a final look in the mirror. Behind me on the bed, Missy's green binder seems to glow, like the old books Hannah and I found in the library. How can I resist?

I flip the cover open. The photographs are still bright, though the plastic sheets have yellowed over the years. In the first picture someone – it must be Mary – pushes a pram along a crowded London pavement, beaming proudly.

There's another picture taken at a playground – a toddler with a crooked fringe wearing dirty yellow dungarees – me!

Hannah shouts up the staircase. 'We'll be late if you don't hurry, Mads.' I'm still just Maddy to her, and Jordan and Darsh.

I close the book and unwrap the parcel. Inside a small box, shrouded in blue tissue paper, is a shiny brass figurine of St Michael, Archangel and Protector.

'This had better be worth the wait!' Hannah calls.

I pop St Michael into my blazer pocket and head down the stairs. I glide noiselessly, as if that ghostly cushion was back, keeping my footsteps graceful and light.

I wait for a few seconds, protected by the corridor's archway. All the girls will be waiting, including Natalie Ashmore. What if they laugh at me? Of course, they'll laugh – at least Nat will. And then what?

'Come on, Mads. We can't take the suspense.'

I take a deep breath, hold my head up, step on to the floor and turn into the corridor.

'Oh – my – goodness,' Hannah gasps. 'Flaming red – you weren't kidding.'

Nat Ashmore steps back as if she's been dazzled by a bright light. Then she tilts her head, leaning closer, squinting to get a proper view. She looks at the other girls, who are waiting for her judgement.

'That's not bad, you know,' she says.

'Not bad?' Hannah squeals. 'Oh, Maddy – you are awesome.'

Hannah takes my arm, and we leave Natalie and her mates to trail in our wake. I'm led like a conquering hero on to the mezzanine, where the boys are filtering in from their rooms. When they see me they all turn and stare – Jake Coates' mouth is open in astonishment. Does he even recognise the new me? Do I recognise myself?

Inside my bag, my mobile hums and vibrates. I stop at the top of the stairs, reach into the front pocket.

It's Caleb calling from London.

'Hey,' I say, turning sideways, letting the others pass me as they charge down the stairs.

'So are the rumours true?' Caleb laughs.

'What rumours – what have you heard?'

I look down at the entrance hall. Everyone – the girls, the boys, even Jordan and Darshan – is gazing up at me. Is it the new hair, I wonder? The make-up?

Or is it something more?

'I've heard there's a new girl at Crowham,' Caleb says.

I put my hand in my pocket and feel the St Michael figure – the sharp sword, the solid armour.

Hannah waves from the bottom of the stairs. 'Come on, Mads. We're all waiting for you.'

I hurry down the steps to join my friends.

'Yes,' I tell Caleb. 'I think there might be.'

My dearest sisters and loving brother,

I thank thee most heartily for thy letters of warning, bidding me beware the tempter's snare, admonishing me to heed not the foul and empty promises of the fiend.

You call him demon. Destroyer of good.

You, who cower from the realms of passion, who have never felt love's joyous sting.

Listen—canst thou not hear the sound that rises above the howling wind, the snarling trees, the fluttering of flames?

Though the night be wild with thunderous storms, there comes a knock upon the door. The gentlest of taps...

It is he—the one you call devil.

Soon I will open the door unto him, and thereafter, we shall never be parted. Not tonight. Not tomorrow.

Never, my dear ones.

Never, ever.

Alice Deeprose

AUTHOR'S NOTE

The Crowham Martyrs is a work of fiction and was never meant to be accurate in terms of the background to events in the story. As Mr Casey says, you won't read about the Crowham Martyrs in any history book!

It's estimated (though figures vary) that during the 16th and 17th centuries 1,000 people, were executed for witchcraft in England and its American colonies. In Scotland, the number was significantly higher, with some historians estimating that over 3,000 were killed. The total figures for Europe are unimaginable, with estimated numbers ranging from 50,000 to hundreds of thousands.

In the county of Sussex, however, only one woman was executed for being a witch. She lived in the village of Kirdford, near Horsham, and was convicted of witchcraft and sentenced to death 1575. Her name was Margaret Cooper.

ACKNOWLEDGEMENTS

First of all, I would like to thank my amazing agent, Sallyanne Sweeney. Her unstinting belief in this story, and in me, have been inspiring and encouraging every step of the way.

Thanks, too, to the wonderful Liz Bankes at Catnip, for her insightful editorial vision, as well as her enthusiasm and support.

I can't thank these brilliant (and beautiful) women enough!

I'm also extremely grateful to Pip Johnson, for the most perfect cover I could have wished for, and for the support of Robert Snuggs and all the lovely people at Bounce Sales and Marketing.

This book also wouldn't have been possible without the continuing support of my writing colleagues, especially my fellow SCBWI members. Once again, I'd like to express my gratitude to everyone involved with Undiscovered Voices 2010, which opened so many doors for me.

Thanks to Helen Sharples for 'bosoms bristling' and Racheal Crowther for 'perm protectors'. I don't want to be accused of plagiarising those fantastic phrases, and I'm so delighted they found their way into print!

And, lastly, to my wonderful children, Sean and Hannah, to whom this book is dedicated, and the many family and friends who've helped me keep things on course. Luckily for me, there are too many of you to mention by name, but I thank you all from the bottom of my heart.

www.catnippublishing.co.uk